If I were the only girl in the world,
and you were the only prince ... (ribbit) !

Tyne O'Connell lives in a tragically small flat in Mayfair, London, where she argues with a temperamental laptop, Nancy Mitford, by day and parties like a wild thing by night. She has written six published humorous adult novels, articles for *Marie Claire*, *Vogue*, *Elle* and that sort of thing. She loved her all-girls convent school so much that all three of her children ran away to boarding school to find out if it really was that cool and decided it was. Tyne always fancied herself as a bit of a fencer, but mostly she fancied boys who fenced. She urged all her children to try a little fencing, and her eldest son was one of the top sabreurs in the under-sixteens in Britain. She still loves sleepover parties (the sort where no one sleeps), as her fourteen-year-old daughter knows only too well . . .

Duelling Princes

THE CALYPSO CHRONICLES

by Tyne O'Connell

Piccadilly Press • London

First published in Great Britain in 2006
by Piccadilly Press Ltd.,
5 Castle Road, London NW1 8PR
www.piccadillypress.co.uk

First published in the USA by Bloomsbury Children's Books

A catalogue record for this book is available from the British Library

ISBN: 1 85340 898 0 (trade paperback)
EAN: 9 781853 408984

3 5 7 9 10 8 6 4 2

Printed and bound in Great Britain by Bookmarque Ltd
Cover design by Fielding Design and Sue Hellard
Designed by M Rules based on an original design
by Louise Millar

Set in Adobe Caslon, Arial and Pike

*To my daughter and muse, Her Royal Stunningness,
Cordelia O'Connell, and my son, the most distressingly
fit boy to ever wield a sabre, Zad Santospirito.
I kiss my blade and salute you both.*

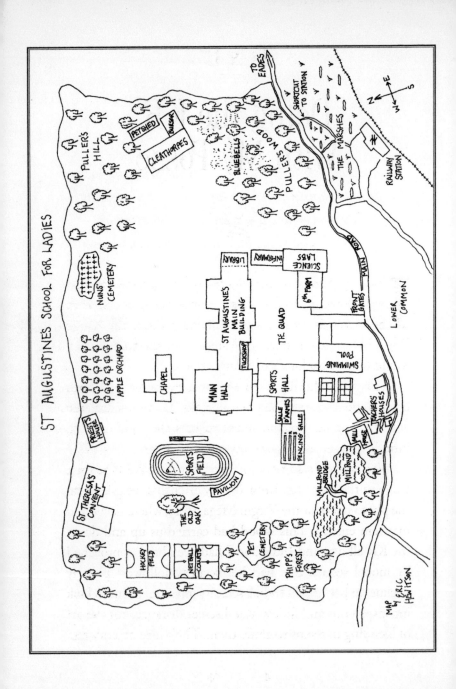

ONE

Doing the KR
With My Posse

I had my head out the window of the car and my hair was blowing about my face – only not so much as to blow my tiara off – as we cabbed it down the King's Road. We were en route to Waterloo for the train, which would take us back to Saint Augustine's.

'This has officially been *the* most awesome half-term break in the history of half-term breaks,' Georgina declared with that grand English drawl of hers that had once so intimidated me as she gave my hand a squeeze.

We'd bought said tiara for two pounds at Ad Hoc for a laugh in the morning. Immediately after that we piled into the photo booth at the Virgin Mega Store, where havoc and mayhem ensued. This mood had carried us up and down the KR all day, and Indie and I had even been approached by model scouts. She had her security followers politely decline on her behalf. Indie's security guys are meant to look inconspicuous and follow at a discreet distance, but the art of blending in seems to elude them. Their idea of a discreet distance and Indie's are about ten metres apart from each other. Indie is a *real* princess, with her own kingdom, personal zoo and everything, but she's not a bit affected. 'They approach me all the time, darling,' she groaned as the nice model scout was being despatched. 'They can be soooo annoying, don't you think?' she asked, grabbing my arm before it had a chance to greedily snatch at the business cards the model scout was begging us to take 'just in case'.

I rolled my eyes as if I knew exactly what she meant, when inside I was excited that a real model scout had just approached me and said I had the look they were looking for!

I'm not surprised they approach Indie all the time. She is the most beautiful girl I know. She looks like a young Naomi Campbell. I suppose Indie is right, though; the last thing I would want to be is a model because it means basing your entire life on your body image. Plus the camera puts ten pounds on you. And then, one day, when you don't have 'the look' any more, your body image must go to pot.

Indie had bought the tiara for me as I was paying for a pair of gorgeous green sequined slippers, turned up at the toe, to replace my Hello Kitty ones. Yes, I had reached that benchmark point when it was time to say a fond farewell to my Hello Kitty stage and leave that innocent babyish period of my life behind. Of course there would be a certain amount of regret and there would always be a place in my heart for Hello Kitty. I would never give up my Hello Kitty toaster back at home in LA because it toasts little Hello Kitty faces on your bread. It was just that at fifteen – well, two months off anyway – I felt it was time to feng shui my life. To make way for more, well, for more grown-up-ish pursuits. Like boys.

'Now that you've pulled your prince you'll be needing a crown, darling,' Indie had teased in a nice piss-take of my American accent, plonking the ghastly purple plastic tiara on my head. Once I would have been too embarrassed to walk down the street in a tiara covered in fake jewels. Even when I was a little girl playing fairies, dressing up always embarrassed me – mostly because my parents had this little stage built in the living room with curtains and all the trimmings. I'd have to give performances for my two adoring fans who cheered and carried on like I was a superstar.

Can I just say, and I think I speak for a lot of only children here, it's really, really hard being the object of all that parental love. Bob, that's what my father likes me to call him, explained he was only trying to support my creative endeavours. Given that my creative endeavours at age five were, for the most part, focused on trying to get my mud pies to taste like chocolate and to defy gravity and fly, all the stages and curtains in the world weren't going to help me, were they? When I have children, I'll be much more restrained than Sarah and Bob are with me. I'll be reasonable and sane and let my children call me Mummy or Mom, like normal children. Mind you, I am soooo glad that I am NOT a grown-up, because as far as I can tell, being a grown-up sucks big-time.

Anyway, while I didn't say anything to my friends, I couldn't help this feeling that I had finally arrived. OK, so I wasn't a Trustafarian, or a real princess, and the car packed with security guys discreetly following us wasn't for *my* protection, but I was here. I was on the King's Road, that HQ of Sloaneishness where all public school girls and boys go to burn Daddy's plastic, parade with their posses, and meet one another.

By the way, public schools in England are the opposite of public schools in America. They are ancient grand places where the great and the good parents send their children from age eleven (or seven even) to learn what it is to be great and good. My parents are good but not what you'd call great. They packed me off at age eleven to Saint Augustine's School for Young Ladies because my mother, Sarah, went there and said it was super. My father's American, but he always goes along with whatever Sarah thinks – actually I think they think with one mind, they are such clones of one another. My first three years at public school in England really sucked (apart from having Star as a best friend). But since working out how the system operates and pulling boys (well, one boy in particular, Prince Freddie, heir to the throne of Great Britain) my life has really been looking up.

If you ever want to go public-school-pupil spotting, the King's Road is *the* place to go. You can do the Ken High (Kensington High Street) as well, but it's not quite in the same league. The long, narrow traffic-choked street of mostly Georgian buildings that runs from Sloane Square to World's End, with its boutique shops and chichi High Street brands, is a Mecca for attendees of public school.

'Well,' as Star says, 'we need some sort of meeting place when we're locked up in our boarding schools like prisoners most of the year, don't we?'

The last time I'd done the KR with Georgina and Star, I still hadn't shaken my insecurities about being an American outsider taking an illicit peek at a parallel universe. A universe of privileged girls and boys, their names all listed in *Debrett's Peerage and Baronetage* or, if European, the *Almanach de Gotha* – proving they are someone of stature. You can scan yourself blind poring over *Debrett's* and the *Almanach*, but you won't find a Calypso Kelly listed. But these girls and boys, armed with their Trustafarian credentials, rule this part of London, ever mindful that one day they would in all likelihood rule the world.

As Star has always opined in a wonderful piss-take of her own class, 'Their sort always travel in packs, darling. *Quelle horreur* that a posh teen be seen out on her own. No, no, no. You never go anywhere without your posse, daaarling.' Star is rock-star royalty, which is virtually the same as real royalty these days. But even if she weren't royal, Star is bursting with an energy and self-assurance that doesn't acknowledge obstacles.

You can always recognise the public school tribes by their clothes: pashminas, short skirts or jeans, and long, glossy designer-blond tresses for the girls. Ralph Lauren shirts, thin jumpers, and chinos or Levi's for the boys. Sunglasses, if worn, are sported on the back of the head, darling, not the front. The girls will all be calling one another daaarling as they air-kiss members of their extended circle in greeting, or furiously text the friends they are already with on their mobile phones. The boys will be laughing loudly with their mateage, listening to their iPods and flicking butts. For some reason they always smoke their cigarettes right down to the filter, if not beyond.

I've watched these tribes since I first came to England – the way an anthropologist might observe another culture – and even though I would never have admitted it until a year ago, I had longed more than anything to be like them. Up until last summer, that had seemed an utterly impossible task for an American Freak brim full of insecurities and paranoia like me. But that was then. It seemed a long, long time ago too, because now I *am* one of them. Properly one of them. I had scaled the castle walls (only not literally, because I'm rubbish at climbing and scared of heights) and pulled one of their own – the heir to the British throne, Prince Freddie. Freds to me. *My* Freds. Just thinking about him made me glow.

In fact, apart from the Daddy's plastic issue – my daddy doesn't believe in plastic – you couldn't tell me apart from the rest of the KR Sloanes on parade that day, and believe me they were all out in force because it was the last day of half-term. I was there with my own posse – Georgina (George), Star, Indie and the rabbit George and I own together, Dorothy Parker. We'd been very popular strolling down the KR with our pink bunny, who is breathtakingly cute. Everyone we met stopped us to chat and stroke her, apart from the horrible people in Pizza Express Pheasantry, who wouldn't let us in, even with Dorothy in her pet carrier case!

The pimply maître d' had muttered something lame about health and safety regulations but was totally rinsed by Star before the word 'safety' was safely out of his prissy mouth.

'How *dare* you,' Star had railed. 'There's more intelligence in this rabbit's ear than all your pizza dough brains put together!'

Star can get very worked up if anyone threatens our rabbit's rights. Indie, George and I managed to calm her down and drag her off before she could throw the maître d' in the pizza oven. Star can get very passionate about things, which is one of the million reasons she's my best friend. Apart from Pizza Express, though, all the other non-food shops had insisted we let Dorothy have a little hop on the counter and asked to stroke her and ooohed and aaahed.

'She's got star quality,' Indie explained earnestly as she twisted one of her braids seductively at this fit guy who worked in the New Age shop where we all had our astrology charts done. You could tell the guy was mesmerised by her beauty; even I was mesmerised by it.

When he told us that her Jupiter was trined with her Mercury or something mad like that, Star announced in a bored sort of way, 'I always suspected that, daaarling!' and even the fit astrology guy laughed.

Seriously, it was a perfect day, just like in that song by that . . . that person, you know, thingamee whatsit, the one who sang, 'It's such a perfect day', or something like that. I just couldn't wipe the smile off my soul as the cab edged its way slowly from light to light. I arranged my tiara and wondered what Freds was doing for a moment, before stopping myself. I am determined to be one of those wildly cool girls who doesn't scramble her brains, texting and obsessing about her boyfriend all the time and neglecting her school-work and her fencing. Especially my fencing, because I have *four* tournaments coming up where FIE judges, BFA scouts and other important people of the fencing world will be watching my every move with eagle eyes. If I did well, I might be invited to join the National Team. I was feverish with hope.

No. As lovely and princely as Freddie is, I was going to be madly cool and mentally collected about our relationship. Even though that would be very difficult because my lips were still quite puffy from all the kissing we'd been doing the day before, and he is the most distressingly fit boy in all the world. Oh, the bliss! When we weren't quad bike riding around Star's estate, we had barely drawn breath. Not just because of all our kissing but because we couldn't stop talking. I find everything about him interesting and extraordinary, and here's the maddest thing of all: he says the same about me! On Tuesday he said I was the most exotic creature he'd ever met. It was soooo cool that I was quite literally gob-smacked, meaning I couldn't even blurt something stupid back like I normally would.

He had gone back home to Balmoral or one of his other famous ancient castles. I wasn't really paying attention to what he was saying, it was just so mesmerising watching the way his lips moved when he spoke. And what are words to soul mates anyway?

It's true, apart from being the fittest boy God ever

breathed life into, Freddie kisses like, well . . . like a very good kisser. In America we say hot! Thank goodness he isn't like those sloppy kissers you see on movies that look like they want to swallow one another's faces and make slurpy slushy noises with their saliva. Star had a sloppy kisser at her house party. I think he was from the village. Clemmie pulled him and then regretted it because his lips roamed all over her face. Luckily Star spotted him and pulled him off to her father's chill room, where Jim Beam pours out of an angel of death fountain on to a Japanese rock pool.

Star's father, being a madly famous rock star, has made their whole house an homage to the rock-and-roll lifestyle as seen on MTV's *Cribs*. I love staying with Star, and even my stricter-than-thou parents are cool with it on account of how Bob is a huge fan of Dirge – that's Tiger's band. Tiger is Star's father and, even though he's perpetually stoned and calls everyone 'man' and goes into unconscious stupors on the floor so that you have to step over him to get your breakfast, he's wildly cool. As Star says, 'He's incredibly bright and wise occasionally, you know, when he's more or less conscious.'

But back to Freddie, he of the glossy, short sticky-up black hair that doesn't need gel or mousse to make it gorgeous. Freddie of the smooth, long-fingered hands and soft lips – well, you get the picture, FIT – although I explained to my mother that he was HOT in fear of her thinking he was some sort of exercise steroid-taking freak. Even though he will one day be the King of the United Kingdom, he's not in the least bit grand or pretentious about it. He sends me lovely text messages all the time and, although he hasn't said anything official, I just know he's serious by the way he supports my neck when he kisses me and smells all lemony.

After living in England for four years I am fully aware that the term 'dating' is considered gauche by the English, and to use it would make one the object of derision and disgust. No one here does dates. They catch up, meet up, see one another and pull – pull like no other nation on earth. But the word 'dating' isn't in their lexicon. So while Freds and I are not actually 'dating', it's sort of understood that we are boyfriend and girlfriend – especially after the half-term week which we spent quad biking around Star's enormous Derbyshire estate, nearly pulling one another's lips off and micro-studying one another's backgrounds.

And even though half-term had now sadly come to an end, Star, George, Indie and I were going out on a high. Or at least we were until Star spotted Ed, the boy Indie had pulled at Star's house party, talking to some girls from Cheltenham. We could tell they were from Cheltenham because . . . well . . . because of the subtle tribal things that suggested it.

'Darling, check out Eds and his mateage,' yelled Star as we were stalled at the traffic lights. 'Who *are* those Cheltenham slappers he's talking to?'

Without anything needing to be said, we all stuck our heads out the window and hissed and jeered. Then, just as Eds turned around, we bobbed on the floor of the cab so he wouldn't see us. We hated Cheltenham girls, for, erm, well,

because they are . . . OK, for no particular reason whatso-
ever, actually. Apart from the fact that they aren't Saint
Augustine girls. And how dare they fraternise with Eds,
whom the most stunning girl in our year had pulled and
text-flirted with relentlessly all break!

Indie was texting furiously before we'd even wound the
window up, which we did because it was autumn and
bloody freezing and we were all wearing the skimpiest
clothes we could feasibly get away with without dying of
hypothermia. 'How *dare* he!' she said with a fearsome
amount of feeling. 'Bloody boys. I am soooo never, never,
never . . .' she ranted before running out of steam.

'What are you going to say to him?' Star asked, looking
slightly worried. Indie can get quite hotheaded – just like
Star, really.

WHO THE HELL ARE YOU TALKING TO AND WHY THE FRUUP
DIDN'T YOU TELL ME YOU WERE ON THE KR? She held up her
phone so we could read the words for ourselves. Then she
pressed 'Send' before we could discuss the matter further.

'But he might know them!' I blurted. That's what I do:
blurt things like that when emotions are running high and
the last thing people want to hear is my blurt, even if it is
vaguely reasonable. I don't know why I do it. Bob, who is
soooo PC and wholemeal it's a wonder he hasn't turned
into a bowl of granola, says I need to be more grounded.
He's very big on grounding, is Bob, bless him. But seriously, for all their mad liberal ideas, I really do love my
parents and miss them dreadfully when I'm over here at
school.

I'd sent Bob and Sarah loads of e-mails during half-term break, but I hadn't heard much back, which was unusual because they are normally delirious e-mailers. For all their foibles and mad LA theories, I am rather proud of my parents for being so kind and lovely and obsessed with me. Of course, we've had our ups and downs, but compared to lots of my friend's parents, like poor Georgina, whose father ran off with someone called Koo-Koo and barely ever sees her, Bob and Sarah are totally cool. And more important, they are always there for me.

'Well he can bloody well *un*-know them,' Indie said, replying to my reasonable suggestion about Eds – only she was smiling as she said it. Indie is fearsome when she's cross. Thank goodness she's never been cross with me. Yet.

'Well, I didn't like the look of them,' Star told her supportively as we climbed off the floor of the cab and sat back up on the seats. 'They looked very slutty to me.'

'Nor did Dorothy,' added Georgina. 'Madly unimpressed,' she told us as she held Dorothy up so we could inspect her unimpressed expression. I suspect Dorothy was just cross because she hates going in cars, but Indie was sold. She rubbed her nose against Dorothy's.

'Dorothy, you are soooo wise. If you say I should dump Eds here and now, I will. Wiggle your nose for "no" and flap your ears for "yes", OK?'

Dorothy wiggled her nose, but actually I don't think she's ever flapped her floppity ears in all her life, and I think Indie knows that very well.

A text alert sounded, but it wasn't Indie's, so a mad

scramble through tiny handbags for still tinier mobiles ensued, which resulted in all our handbags being emptied on the floor of the cab.

It was mine.

MISSING U ALRDY. I'VE GOT A GORG PHOTO OF U ON MY LAPTOP. U R DISTRESSINGLY STUNNING KELLY. NO WONDER SCOUTS R AFTER U! FREDS XXX

How sweet and psychic was that? I bet our planets were trined. I'd only seen him, well, the day before, actually, and already he was missing me. He had to go to some shoot thingamee. Most of my friends like shooting things, apart from Star. She's a mad *anti*, only she can get away with it because she's a proper rock royalty eccentric. Unlike me, who's just an opinionated PC liberal American with misguided opinions about field sports and country pursuits, which is what the English call killing foxes, grouse, deer and pheasants.

Freddie had been very sweet when I'd lectured him about the killing of things wild and winged. He ruffled my hair and kissed my nose and promised to try and aim poorly. I hoped that he'd just aimed poorly, remembered me, and sent me the text. How wildly romantic would that be?

I had the best boyfriend in the world. I had to keep pinching myself to stop screaming it out loud at the top of my lungs for all the world to hear.

MISSING YOU TOO, XXXX C I typed into my mobile before thinking better of it and changing the four x's to three.

MISSING YOU TOO, XXX C – yes, that was much better. If he sent me three kisses, I should follow suit. I didn't want him to think I was planning our wedding or something tragic like that.

Then I added a PS: HOPE YOU ARE MISSING ALL THINGS WINGED TOO!

His response was immediate. WANT TO MEET UP IN WINDSOR ON SAT? F XXX

I didn't need to even think about my answer.

DEFS! XXX C

TWO

'Rental Meltdown

Back at school we all clambered up the narrow, dimly-lit, ancient stairs of the main building of Saint Augustine's. I was rushing a bit, keen to get back to my own dorm room to catch up with my roommate Portia, so we could stress out and strategise about our upcoming fencing tournaments.

Portia and I have had our ups and downs, but the downs were mostly my fault, like, well, erm, wrongfully accusing her of trying to steal Freds. I know now that my suspicions were mad, especially as she was actually pulling Billy, the captain of the Eades fencing team. But we'd made up and were now very much on an up. Portia was as keen as me to distinguish herself at the Nationals, but before that, we had our regionals and three other tournaments to place second or first in if we were to get ourselves noticed by the scouts for the National team. Over the coming weeks we'd have to have our sabres practically glued to our hands.

I heard voices in my room, which made me curious, as apart from Lady Portia Herrington Briggs (not that she was so tragic as to use her title), my only other roomie was the

Honorable Honey O'Hare (who has her title written on her stationery). Portia and Honey barely maintain civilities. But as I entered the room I had a hallucination and completely missed my bed, falling instead in a heap on the floor.

'Whoops-a-daisy,' my mother, Sarah, said in a baby voice and laughed.

Yes, my mother, Sarah Kelly, who should have been tucked up in Hollywood with my father, Bob, eating granola, reading *Variety* magazine and bemoaning the lack of art house and foreign movies up for awards these days. I wish it had been a hallucination, but no, it really *was* my mother, in all her wholemeal glory, sitting on my bed as large as life.

'Come and give your mumsy-wumsy a huggle, Boojie.' Her accent was halfway between Freddie's mother's and Hillary Clinton – a bit like Madonna used to sound when she was going through her Anglophile stage.

And what was with the baby-talk?

Honey, who was pretending innocently to listen to her iPod, started making the noise she makes when she laughs – sort of like a hog snuffling through rubbish. She can't actually laugh because she's had soooo much Botox she'd run a serious risk of botulism poisoning.

'What are you doing here, Sarah?' I demanded, climbing off the floor.

'I've run away,' she said, as if she really were a little girl who'd run away.

'Run away? Run away from what?' I felt like adding 'at your age?' but I held back.

'Rents are such hypocrites – if I were to run away, they'd

track me down, probably with tracker dogs and social workers, and lecture me from here to eternity. I felt like giving Sarah a lecture and telling her what a naughty madam she was and how she was going to be grounded for life – only not here in my dorm, obviously. They don't condone the presence of parents at Saint Augustine's apart from on speech day or at Sunday Mass.

I gave her a very, very, very stern look before realising I was still wearing my tiara. I chucked it on my bedside table. I needed to be taken seriously, and a purple tiara would limit my aspirations in that department.

'What do you mean, "run away"? You can't run away, Sarah. What will Bob do without you?'

'Humph!' was her response to that. 'It's your father I've run away from, Calypso.'

'My father?' I asked, realising this was bad. Sarah had never called Bob 'your father' before. That's how divorced parents talk in movies. But then my parents do live in Hollywood.

'Yes, your father. Bob and his Big One. Oh, Calypso, I've had it up to here with his Big One!' she cried, holding her hand several inches above her head to demonstrate.

More smirks from Honey.

'You know what he's like. All he's gone on about these past two years is his Big One. I supported him all this time in his creative endeavour, but the last month has been intolerable. He's barely surfaced from his study. And then when I told him I'd had it up to here,' – she held her hand above her head again – 'he asked me if I wanted him to trade his soul for an unfulfilling job on some godawful soap like me! Well, that's it! Finito! My godawful soap has supported us all these years, so I told him to take his Big One and shove it where the sun don't shine.'

I looked over at Portia. Her inscrutable, dark, long-lashed eyes were bug-eyed with horror – only I couldn't be sure what she was horrified by exactly.

'It's his script,' I explained hastily, lest she think my father's Big One was, well, you know what. 'He's writing his Big One, the script that will carve his name in cinematic history.'

'And currently brings in no money,' Sarah added pointedly. 'Can you believe it, girls?' Sarah asked, playing to her audience. 'Well, I packed my bags and decided to come where I was appreciated – here.'

'But you can't stay here, Sarah!' I told her, horrified.

The girls looked at each other, no doubt embarrassed for me. Parents in England don't share their problems with their offspring – well, not in my world. But Sarah was oblivious to her audience's discomfort as she wiped a tear from her eye.

'I mean, they don't let grown-ups stay in dorms,' I said.

'I don't mean *here*. I mean the land of my birth.'

'But Sarah, are you sure? I mean, Bob can't pack in a script he's been working on for so long. He told me he had almost finished it and besides, he does get *some* money from the Writers' Guild, and you *were* the one who insisted he chuck his perfectly good job and focus his genius on his creative endeavours,' I reminded her.

'Yes, well that was before I knew his creative endeavours

were going to take so long. No, I discussed it with Bunny. And last week I made the decision I should have made years ago and put my plan to leave into action. I've come home to London to be with you!'

OK, this was officially serious. Images of a frantic Bob pacing madly in search of his other half flashed through my mind. And who was Bunny? 'Did you tell him you were leaving?' I asked, my voice showing my panic. 'He's probably beside himself with worry!'

'Huh!' Sarah brushed this idea aside with a wave of her hand. I noticed she was still wearing her wedding ring at least. 'He probably hasn't even noticed I've gone. Last time I saw him he had his head bent over his laptop and was waving away the dim sum I'd brought him for supper, you know the ones he loves with the . . .'

And that was when it got seriously scary. Her lower lip wobbled, she stretched out her arms for me to fall into and, reverting back to baby-talk, added, 'Bunny's right. At least I'll get to spend more quality time with my Boojie-woojems.'

'Boojie-woojems,' Honey mimicked. This time she *did* laugh, and her collagen-enhanced lips looked ready to explode with the mirth of it all.

See, this proves the absurdity of 'rentals. You love them, you put up with their unreasonable demands, you patiently endure their weird food fads and cultural oddities. For years, you even obey them slavishly and look up to them like they're veritable gods, but ultimately you start seeing through the disguise, right into the insanity and hypocrisy of who they *really* are.

For starters, it was Sarah's idea to pack me off to boarding school when I was eleven, promising me how it would be 'super' and how 'you'll make friends for life' when for three and a half years it wasn't a bit 'super'. It was a nightmare. And now that I actually *was* having a 'super' time and making friends for life, my mother pitches up and calls me a name she hasn't called me since I was five and starts ranting about my father's Big One. It's perverse, that's what it is. Even all this guff about Bob and his Big One, that was her idea too! She was the one who persuaded him to chuck his decent job at Warner and concentrate on his script. OK, it was taking him a lot longer than she'd probably imagined, but still!

Portia was looking at me sympathetically, or perhaps it was a look of helpless pity – the sort of look you give to mad teachers.

'But surely you and Bob will work this out? You love each other. Who'll finish off Bob's sentences if you're not there?' I reasoned, stroking her hair like she was the child and I was the grown-up. 'And who is Bunny?'

'Oh, Boojie . . .' she said in a slightly hysterical baby-voice as she attempted to wrap me in a cuddle.

I wriggled away from her. 'Can you stop calling me *that*!' I snapped.

Sarah looked as if I'd struck her, and I immediately felt bad.

The room fell silent for a bit. I could hear the *tap, tap, tap* of our House Spinster Miss Bibsmore's stick as she wandered down the corridor on her rounds, when suddenly

Sarah began to sob, big heart-wrenching sobs. Portia gave her a tissue and I wrapped my mother in a big daughterly cuddle.

'Bob's Big One, what a joke!' my mother remarked sarcastically.

'Sarah, you've soooo got to stop saying that,' I pleaded with her under my breath, handing her another tissue.

'Saying what?' she asked innocently as she dabbed at her mascara-daubed panda eyes.

'Well . . . you know, Bob's Big One. People might think, well, they might get the wrong idea about what the Big One *is*, if you see what I mean.'

'You mean the big earthquake? Well, they'd be right, because this all feels pretty damn cataclysmic to me.'

I didn't know what she was talking about for a minute, but then I remembered that Los Angeles is on a fault line.

'I thought you left him because his penis is too small, darling,' Honey said, fluttering her eyelashes, which were almost long enough to do herself an injury.

Sarah looked momentarily horrified by what Honey had just said, but then she started to cry again, not in a sobbing, wrenching way, though, but more in a crumpled little girl sort of way, which made me feel even more helpless. Honey started dialling someone on her phone.

'Oh my gawd, darling, you have got to get down here and fast. The American Freak's mother's turned up. She's a bigger freak than *her*. She's clearly from a long line of ancestral freakage . . .' This was rich coming from a girl who only two weeks ago was gadding about with an iron beak on her nose.

I grabbed her phone and threw it across the room. 'Get out,' I told her with an authority I barely knew I had off the fencing piste.

'*You* can't talk to *me* like that!' she shrieked, flicking her long, blond, expensively-streaked and straightened hair over her skinny, tanned shoulders.

'Just leave now,' Portia added in her grandly aloof way, and Honey, seeing herself outnumbered, retrieved her phone and sauntered into the corridor, checking her reflection in her Chanel compact as if it had been her own idea to ban herself from her own dorm room. For those of you who've not met Honey, she's not the sort of girl to miss a scandal – she's the sort of girl to start one.

'Look, I'm sure it's just a bit of a tiff,' I soothed, rubbing Sarah's back, unsure of what to do or say. I gave her a cuddle, and as I wrapped my arms around her I noticed some strands of grey hair mixed in with her lovely natural fair hair.

She struggled free. 'A tiff? A tiff? Is that what you think this is? Do you think I'm so shallow that I'd walk out on the man I love over a tiff?'

Stupid, stupid, stupid Calypso! Why did I blurt that stupid word 'tiff'? It sounded like a cleaning product. I slapped my forehead. 'Sorry, I didn't mean to say that. But if you love him, why –'

But Sarah was on a roll. 'You try living with a man who's self-absorbed in an ever-growing mountain of script. I hardly ever see him. And he's making *no* money, as I was just explaining to Portia earlier. *I'm* holding everything together.'

'Well, you can't hold things together if you're here, though, can you?' I reasoned.

'Yes, I can. Remember I am still a British citizen,' she said, holding herself upright in an imperious sort of way. For a moment I feared she was about to burst into a chorus of 'God Save the Queen'. 'I've got a job on *Gladesdale* in fact.'

'*Gladesdale?*' *Gladesdale* was probably the chaviest programme on television, a sort of bad soap opera for teens.

'And taken a house in Clapham.'

'Clapham!' I yelped. Clapham was *not* a place girls from Saint Augustine's spoke of. Clapham was where people who couldn't afford a big house in Chelsea lived in delusional gentrification and, more importantly, it was south of the river, and south of the river soooo wasn't part of my friends' world. Between *Gladesdale* and Clapham, I was going to be massacred.

I could hear Honey giggling in the corridor. She shrieked out the words 'Clapham' and '*Gladesdale*' with the relish of a hound dog baying for blood. The writing was already on the wall for me now. From this moment forth I would be known as the Girl from Clapham, or probably the Clap, for short. And just when things were going so well.

Sarah hugged me to her tiny bosom. 'Won't it be lovely to see more of one another, darling? You can have sleepover parties with your friends. I can buy marshmallows and fish and chips.'

I tried to smile back. 'Sarah, I'm not five any more, and

the next few weeks are really, really busy for me. I've got the Nationals and before that the Regionals and as well as that I've got three other tournaments. And GCSEs to study for.'

Miss Bibsmore's *tap, tap, tapping* was drawing closer.

'Oh, I see. So what you're saying is, you'd rather I go back to Bob and his Big One and live in a perpetual twilight of unhappiness?' my mother asked as a solitary tear ran down her mascara-stained cheek.

'Yes,' I blurted before I had time to shove my pillow in my mouth. 'No, of course not. I meant no. No, that is, I don't want you to live in a perpetual twilight of unhappiness, but, well, I don't want you and Bob to break up, do I? You guys love each other. You said so yourself.'

'Ha!' my mother scoffed. 'Callow youth. What do you know about love?'

I managed to stop myself from saying, 'Well, quite a lot, actually,' but I did say, 'Sarah, for the last time, will you stop calling his script the Big One! Just call it his, erm, Opus or something.'

'Oh, an' wot 'ave we got 'ere then, eh?' Miss Bibsmore asked, her odd little form leaning on the doorframe, looking none too pleased at the sight of my mother sprawled on the bed.

'Miss Bibsmore, this is my mother. She's, erm, she's visiting from America.'

Miss Bibsmore took in the scene. The panda-eyed, tear-streaked face of my mother, the looks of worry and concern on the faces of Portia and myself, and the shadowy presence of Honey peering in from the corridor. 'Well, I'm pleased to meet you an' all, I'm sure, Mrs Kelly. Miss Kelly 'ere is a good girl, no trouble from her. Not like some,' she added darkly, turning to eye up Honey. 'Always polite is Miss Kelly.'

'How kind of you to say,' my mother replied. 'We tried to teach her manners and, well, I'm an old girl myself, actually.'

Miss Bibsmore put her hands on her hips. 'I'm not old! What do mean coming in 'ere and calling me *old*. I'm in my prime I am, an' all. "Old" indeed!'

'No, no, no, you misunderstood me, Miss Bibsmore,' Sarah said. 'I was a Saint Augustine's girl myself many years ago.'

Miss Bibsmore humphed. 'All the same, be that as it may, it's time for visitors to be off, innit. Parents or no parents. Old girl or not. Rules is rules.'

My mother nodded obediently and gathered up her large handbag and a pale blue pashmina I'd never seen. As she kissed both cheeks she said, 'I'll call you on your cell, but if you need me, this is my number.' She passed across a card with an address and phone number on it.

She already had a card? This was serious. Sarah really *had* left Bob!

She didn't look at me as I took the card, and I felt that I'd failed her somehow. Maybe I should have joined her in attacking Bob and his Big One, but the truth was I just didn't believe something like this could happen to my parents. I gave her a proper cuddle, and the familiar smell of her musky Keils perfume made me feel like crying myself. She seemed so small and I felt so strong and tall as I stroked her hair the way she used to stroke mine.

How could this be happening? How could my good, decent, liberal, loving parents have come to this? Bob and Sarah? Sarah and Bob? Even their names sounded right together. They thought with one mind, their hearts beat to the same political ideological pulse, and they backed one another's madness to the hilt. If that isn't love, I don't know what is.

But now here we were, Bob on one side of the world and Sarah living in Clapham, of all places. I couldn't begin to imagine what Bob was going through. I mean, he can barely pour his own granola without Sarah. I imagined him lying in a heap of despair, living under piles of pizza boxes, too weak to work, too despondent to go on. Surely he'd be on a plane begging her forgiveness and tearing his script to shreds. OK, so there'd be a back-up copy on his computer, but at least it would be a gesture.

Sarah was the love of his life. He was always saying that (much to my embarrassment). He'd even told my head-mistress, Sister Constance. But what if Sarah was right? Maybe he *hadn't* noticed she'd even gone, buried as he was under his, erm, Opus.

Before Sarah left, I agreed to go and see the house in Clapham with her on Saturday. It was the least I could do. It was only after she had said her tearful goodbye that I remembered I'd agreed to see Freds on Saturday. And then I felt conflicted. Was it really shallow of me to put the joy of meeting my boyfriend above spending time with my mother in her time of need? I was pretty sure the answer was yes.

I would have to text Fred, although maybe calling him would be better. I was sure he'd be sympathetic, or was it too early in our relationship for me to start burdening him with personal problems? Oh God, it was all so complicated.

Portia came over and sat on my bed with me. 'I'm really sorry about your parents, Calypso. But I've seen Bob and Sarah together, when they came to the school after Honey sold those photographs of you and Freddie to the tabloids, and –'

'I did *not* sell them,' Honey snapped indignantly, stepping back into the room. 'I just gave them to them. There is a difference you know, it's not as if I needed the money –'

'Oh shut up, Honey. No one was talking to you,' Portia said calmly. 'Seriously, Calypso, I'm sure they'll work it out . . .'

I nodded, because in the summer Portia had seen her mother killed by a car on Sloane Street, and I knew she wasn't just offering polite words of comfort.

'Yes, poor Boojie. But at least you'll have your mumsy close by you in lovely gentrified Clapham,' said Honey as she admired her false talons. 'And just think of all the sleepover parties you can have in *Clapham*. Won't it just be super, darling!' she squealed, in a scarily good piss-take of my mother's accent as she clapped her hands with fake glee. 'I wish I could be more like you, Boojie,' she taunted me.

'Well, why don't you start by helping yourself to a little less Botox – it's clearly gone to your brain,' Star sneered as she entered the room with Indie. 'It's about time you started showing Calypso some respect. She's probably the most talented person you know. She's going to be a writer, and the pen is mightier than the postcode. Apart from writing the lyrics for our album,' – she looked over at Indie and put her finger to her lips – 'she's entering the Interschool Essay Competition. She'll definitely win it,' Star announced with enormous authority. 'They're publishing the best three in the *Telegraph*, Honey.'

'So, why would I care about a sorry little essay?' Honey asked with a little less bravado.

'Because the sorry little essay has to depict personal suffering, and I'd say Calypso has been through quite a lot of personal suffering at your hands, wouldn't you, Honey?'

Honey was uncharacteristically quiet.

It was the first I'd heard about either lyric writing or essay competitions, but I trusted Star and loved the way it had shut Honey up, so I nodded with smug vigour.

Later that night, I crept into Star's room to ask about the competition. She dug about in her drawer and found a pamphlet advertising a prize of one thousand pounds for the best essay. I read and reread the rules. The essay, which had to be three thousand words in length, was to be an autobiographical account of the most painful experience of a teenager's life. The traumas suggested were growing up as a victim of abuse, coming from a broken or violent home, bullying and the struggles of being an immigrant.

I might not be the richest girl in my privileged world, but it *was* a privileged world. And while I was American, I didn't think the judges would rank me highly as a struggling asylum seeker. True, I had faced the toxic trauma of living with Honey, but would Post-it notes slapped on my back classify as serious abuse? Was there anything in my decent, dull life that would bring a tear to the eyes of the judges? No, was the answer.

It was soooo not a competition for me.

But Star was insistent. 'Of course it is. Your writing is brilliant, Calypso.'

'But I've never suffered, well, not in that sort of way,' I told her, pointing to the pamphlet. Then I thought about the problems I was facing. Saturday for example, and how I'd told Freds I'd meet him and how now I was going to have to tell him that my mother had left my father, which would make me the Complicated Girlfriend even if he was really sympathetic. Oh God. Maybe I should think up some elaborate lie about not being able to make it to Windsor.

Star interrupted my problem-solving plans. 'Darling, we've all suffered. Even me, even Honey. Anyway, you do actually come from a broken home now, remember?'

'But I don't want to come from a broken home, Star,' I suddenly cried. And then the floodgates opened, and I couldn't stop crying. 'I don't want Bob and Sarah to split up!'

'It's OK, darling,' she soothed. 'We'll fix it. I promise. Bob and Sarah were made for each other. Even a fool like Honey can see that.'

THREE

The Fascism of
Creative Endeavours

O n Star's suggestion, I fired off an absolute stinker
of an e-mail to Bob. She was of a mind that a
short, sharp shock worked best with men. 'Stick it
to him,' she told me. 'Make him writhe with guilt.' I was
inclined to trust Star on these matters. Whenever her father
went off the rails, her mother wasted no time pulling him
into line. 'Men are blameless, brainless creatures, darling,'
continued Star. 'In my opinion, Sarah's only come out here
to frighten the bejesus out of Bob. You Americans love all
that shock-and-awe business. Sarah's probably counting the
minutes until Bob turns up in England on his white charger
and carries her back to Hollywood. But the truth is that
men are like quad bikes – they need to be driven.'

I decided on a formal tone, which would leave him in no
doubt as to what he needed to do.

Dear Bob,
I am forced to write this unpleasant e-mail because you don't

'believe' in snail mail (although that would have taken longer anyway, and this is an emergency). But I think not believing in snail mail points to a madness within you because snail mail (like plastic) blatantly does exist. All my school life spent over here I have watched the other girls receive post from their parents and lovingly pin it to the pin boards above their beds as a statement to all that their madres and padres love them.

But I digress. The real reason I am writing to you is to insist that you stop this macho obsession you have with writing the Big One and get yourself a nice soul-destroying job like Sarah and the rest of the world have to put up with.

Creative endeavours are all well and good, but not when they come at the cost of the people you love, e.g., Sarah and your daughter (me). Also, I know you wouldn't want to tear asunder what God glued together the day you wed Sarah on that beach in Hawaii. Nor do I mean to sound selfish, but this marital drama has come at a very inconvenient time for me (yes, me, your little girl, whom you said you loved more than life itself). In case you have forgotten, I am trying out for the Nationals, which you once said was all you lived for!

And poor Sarah is beside herself. She thinks you care more about your script than her! I know that isn't true. I know you love her and this is all just a gigantic misunderstanding. I know what you are like when you write. You go into your own world, but in the process you've made Sarah feel like you don't care about her. Also, this script is taking an awfully long time. I'm sure it will be very good and meaningful and you MIGHT even sell it for loads of money, but maybe you should take a break for the sake of your marriage and come to England to show Sarah how much you love her? It is blatantly obvious to everyone that you are made for one another.

The point is you need to nip this in the bud before it goes any further. Sarah has already got a job and is renting a house in CLAPHAM, which, in case you don't know, is where 'the clap' comes from due to the density of prostitutes that once lived there. At least that's what Honey told me and, although she's a compulsive liar, you told me even liars tell the truth sometimes.

Is this what you really want for the mother of your child? Is this what you want for your wife – working on some plebbie show she really, really hates, burying her creative yearnings alive. [I'd made this bit up, as we hadn't actually spoken about her new gig on Gladesdale or her creative yearnings, but I felt it might strike a chord just the same.] Maybe to prove you love her you will have to go back to your old job writing dramadies like *I Hear Laughter*, which I actually think was very good, even though it did win the Worst Dramady Award three seasons running. So just get a job for a bit and make things right with Sarah so she can go home. You must be wondering where the granola is kept by now anyway.

Your loving daughter,

Calypso

I was very pleased with my e-mail. I was convinced it had been both sympathetic and insistent. Star agreed. We had no doubt that Bob would be charging off to his agents to discuss getting back on a new show as a staff writer before he even read my sign-off.

Instead, I'd hardly pressed 'Send' when he e-mailed a response.

Dearest Calypso,

I am shocked by your narrow-minded determination to cast me as the demon in all this. Sarah knows she can come back any time she chooses to. If your mother really loved me she would respect my need to express myself creatively, as she promised to when we made our marriage vows on that beach in Hawaii. I hope you are eating well and working hard. Maybe she just wants to be near you for a bit, have you thought of that?

Love,

Bob

I was gutted. How could he be so obtuse? While I never really thought of my parents as one of the great love stories of our time, I had always imagined that when I grew up and got married I would want a marriage like Sarah and Bob's. Also, I really didn't want to come from a broken home!

My friends were all brilliantly supportive. The next morning at breakfast, as we dunked our croissants and slurped our cereal, Star was still working on me to enter the essay competition. But honestly, my plate was already full with fencing and GCSEs, I told her, and besides, my plan was to get Sarah and Bob back together, which would mean there wouldn't be an essay of heartfelt loss and suffering to write.

'What essay?' Clemmie asked.

'Calypso's entering an essay-writing competition about the agonies of coming from a broken home,' Star announced to the table at large.

I tried to kick her under the table, missed and knocked my shin on the table leg.

'Wow, that is soooo cool,' Clemmie said.

I glared at Star as I rubbed my shin, but she smiled at me sweetly and said, 'Darling, don't get your knickers in a twist. You just said your e-mail didn't work, so maybe the essay-writing competition will be the thing that actually brings Bob and Sarah back together. Imagine how Bob will feel when he reads of the pain his creative endeavours have wrought on his daughter. He'll drop his Big One like a lead balloon and propose to Sarah all over again.'

'Are you really entering that competition, Calypso?' Portia asked as she sat down. 'We're going to have soooo much going on with the Nationals coming up.'

Sometimes I could strangle Star. But then she somehow always redeems herself. She tossed a croissant at me. 'Don't worry, Calypso. I'm sure this break won't stick. Honestly, grown-ups are such drama queens, and I should know. My parents break up all the time. Mummy even has her own suite at Claridges for her fortnightly bolt. She's always leaving Daddy, hoping that it will make him give up weed.' Star shrugged, as one resigned to her parents' foibles. 'But she always comes back, or he always goes to fetch her, because they both know no one else is going to put up with either of them. Bob and Sarah are the same.'

'That's true. Bob and Sarah have never had an individual

thought. They're like one being. You can't have a Bob without a Sarah, it would be like . . . well, like a Bonny without the Clyde.'

'Like toast without marmalade?' Arabella suggested, spreading a large portion of marmalade on her croissant.

'Quite,' agreed Georgina. 'Like Tobias without my vodka stash.'

We all laughed at that, remembering the debacle of a few weeks back when Star's snake, Brian, had tried to swallow Georgina's teddy, Tobias – who, by the way, is a full fee-paying student with the same rights and responsibilities as other students. Anyway, in the process, Brian tore Tobias apart, exposing the stash of vodka Georgina had concealed inside his stuffing. Tobias had been suspended for a week for drinking. Since then Tobias has been seen by teachers and students alike as a bit of a drunk. Georgina had to promise Sister Constance that she would give him a really stern talking to.

'Poor Sarah. I think your father is being absolutely bloody about this Big One,' Indie added, piling the sugar into her tea. 'How long has he been working on it?'

'About two years,' I told her, cringing that I had been responsible for bringing the term 'Big One' into my friends' lexicon. Surely it was worse than 'dating' even? 'But it was Sarah who insisted he pursue his creative endeavour to write his, erm, Opus,' I justified, feeling suddenly defensive on Bob's behalf. He was soooo passionate about his script and, even though it was taking forever to write, I really did admire him for being so committed.

'Well, personally, I think he should toss this madness. I think we should all be supportive of Sarah. It must be ghastly for her to be all alone, starting a new job, living in Clapham.' Indie's lovely model-like features shivered at the very thought.

'Yes, but Bob wants her back,' I told her. 'He thinks she's being unfair to him when he's so close to finishing it,' I explained, paraphrasing Bob's e-mail.

'Piffle,' Indie scoffed.

'Sarah *did* say she'd like you to have a sleepover party,' Portia reminded me. 'That would cheer her up, having a house full of marauding teenagers.'

I gulped my hot chocolate at the thought and started choking, knowing that (in Sarah's mind) a sleepover meant something very different than what it meant to my friends. Sarah would probably bake chocolate biscuits and have us all sitting in a circle, chatting about our innermost thoughts – with her. Unlike the other girls' parents, who all lived in a different wing of their houses, Sarah would want to spend every moment of the night with us.

'So? Let's all go!' piped up Clemmie, who adores parties almost as much as Tobias.

'I'm in,' agreed Arabella. 'Where did you say she was living?'

'Clapham,' Honey announced loudly, slamming her tray down at our table. She made the word 'Clapham' sound like something a dog might cough up.

'Clapham it is, then,' Georgina declared. 'Arabella? Clems? Indie? Star? Portia?'

'Clapham it is,' they all agreed.

'Oh all right, then,' sighed Honey. 'Clapham it is,' she conceded as if she'd even been invited or something.

'I'll see you in class,' Portia said, unfolding her impossibly long legs and standing beside me. 'And I'll meet you during break in the salle, Calypso, yaah?' she confirmed.

'Yaah,' I agreed. 'I hope Bell End is up for getting us into shape,' I mused.

Portia leaned over and lightly kissed my cheek. 'Don't worry, darling. It's Bell End's glory and reputation on the line as much as ours. And don't worry about your parents. I'm sure it's all going to be fine. They're sooo obviously the perfect couple.'

I smiled and said, 'Of course,' because that's what you have to do when people reassure you – make them feel that they've really helped. Especially after everything Portia had been through. Just the same, Bob's e-mail hadn't exactly encouraged me. What if Sarah wasn't overreacting? What if Bob really was being insensitive? It happens to artists. Only a few weeks ago I felt Star was putting her music before me, but then again I am prone to extreme bouts of insecurity. The truth was, I couldn't have felt less confident, but I hoped against hope that Portia was right.

I was just about to say my own laters to the group when my text alert sounded.

WISH IT WAS SAT 2DAY! FREDS XXX

Oh the joy of having a boyfriend to distract you from the horrors and madness of 'rental separations! Suddenly, Bob and his Big One and Sarah's flight to Clapham were the last things on my mind. The 'rentals would just have to grow up and look after themselves. I couldn't be responsible for them *all* my life. Also, I had far more pressing matters to deal with, like registration, clearing up my room, chapel, lessons, fencing and most of all, my lovely, lovely Freds.

There was no way I could enter an essay-writing competition about my personal pain after his text. I was walking on air. And then I remembered I had agreed to meet Sarah *and* Freds on Saturday. Star, who had leaned over to read my text, gave me a look of sympathy because she knew I'd agreed to go to the house with Sarah on Saturday.

'What are you going to do?' she asked.

'Be in two places at once,' I joked, but actually there was nothing funny about it. Whatever I did, two people were going to be hurt – one of them me. The essay suddenly seemed like an increasingly less absurd idea.

FOUR

Bell End Goes Double Bonkers!

B ell End had taken over from our fencing master Professor Sullivan while he took his sabbatical. We'd had our doubts about him initially, just, well, because he was as different from our suave and debonair professor as it is possible to be. His name wasn't really Bell End, it was Mr Wellend, but, because he is a bit of an idiot, Portia and I had started calling him Bell End – which in England is the name for the end of a boy's whatsit. He is loud, brash, coarse and South African, but there was no doubting his determination to whip us into shape. As the only two serious sabreurs, Portia and I were his big hope. At least that was Portia's reasoning.

We entered the salle at lunch to find it empty, though.

'You don't think he's forgotten us?' I asked, plonking myself on a bench. If he didn't turn up, we wouldn't even be able to practise, such is the policy of the British Fencing Association. The school would be fined thousands of pounds.

'I only spoke to him at break, and he was madly wound up about it. We've already got a tournament this Saturday in Sheffield and he said he'd drive us.'

'Oh, that's brilliant!' I squealed with excitement, jumping up and down on the spot. Sarah definitely wouldn't want me to miss a tournament, and Freds would be there too! All my problems would be solved.

'God, no nerves on your side, then?' Portia said, surprised by the level of my excitement.

'Oh God, no, I will be nervous. It's just that, well, we'll get to see Billy and Freds now.'

'Billy definitely,' she agreed, grinning from ear to ear at the prospect of seeing her boyfriend. 'I spoke to him earlier. But I got the impression from him that Freds wasn't going. You know how he loves to visit his gran whenever he can. And with his security situation, Billy reckons Freds might figure it's not worth it. I mean, the tournaments are more preparatory than essential. Also, Sheffield is like a four-hour drive, and while girls are seeded out by three-thirty or so, the boys sometimes don't finish until seven or even later.'

My face fell.

'But darling, don't worry. It will still be a fantastic day out for Sarah.'

'What?'

'Sarah. You had planned to check out her new house in Clapham,' Portia reminded me. 'But she's sure to want to come to the tournament, isn't she?'

I nodded, trying not to betray myself, but there was no more speculation, as that was when we heard Bell End enter the salle. He was laughing like a, well, like a bit of a maniac actually.

'Come on, then, you big girls' blouses (his favourite term for us), git out here and let's see what you're made of,' he called out to us.

We scrambled into our fencing gear and rushed out to the salle. Without a word being spoken, we got straight on to our stretches.

While we stretched and lunged and lunged some more, Bell End (in full fencing gear) roamed the salle, slashing the air with his sabre. His muscular little body was as stiff as a board as he muttered to himself about new world orders and standards being set and met. Portia and I did our best to stop giggling, but we weren't entirely successful.

Then, after ten minutes, he suddenly yelled out, 'Jerzy Pawlowski!' His voice bounced off the walls.

Portia and I stopped our lunges and looked around the salle, expecting to see some crony of Bell End's entering. But no, it was just Bell End being mad.

We went back to our lunges.

'Jerzy Pawlowski!' he yelled again – only louder this time, so that his voice bounced around the walls for a good while longer. 'Greatest sabreur that ever lived!' he yelled so loudly the words echoed back.

It's best to ignore teachers when they start cracking up, otherwise you can end up being showered in blues, or questioned by therapists, or involved in an investigation after they cart them off to the loony bin. I moved on to my supermans, as did Portia.

'Won the world title outright three years in a row, he did! In 1957, '58 and '59. Took the gold in '68 at the Olympics, and with the Polish team he took gold from the Hungarians in '61, '62 and '63.'

I looked at Portia and she looked at me. Our warm-ups were done, and we were awaiting instructions, but all Bell End did was repeat the name 'Jerzy Pawlowski!' over and over again.

It was going to be a bloody nuisance if our fencing master chose now to crack up. We'd never get through to the Nationals. Ignoring Bell End, Portia and I stood quietly, waiting for him to finish.

'Hungary still hasn't recovered.'

'Heavens,' said Portia, just so he knew we were listening.

Bell End harrumphed. 'How many ways of moving forward do you think Jerzy had, eh?'

'Erm . . . one, sir,' I hazarded. I mean, as a sabreur you spend your life practising moving forward. It's the most repetitive exercise you do. Moving forward and then moving forward over and over again. It doesn't take a genius to work out that there's only one way of moving forward . . . and that's, well . . . it's moving forward, basically.

Portia looked at me and raised one eyebrow in that special aristocratic way she has.

'Eight!' Bell End yelled, slashing the air with his sabre. Again, his voice bounced around the salle. His face had gone purple too, like he might be about to have an apoplectic fit. I wasn't sure about Portia, but I was crap at first aid.

'Eight different ways of moving forward,' Bell End declared in his booming South African voice. 'Footwork of a dancer and every way of moving forward cunningly calculated to provoke a different reaction from his opponent, eh? Eh? Eh?'

Clearly a response was required. 'Eight, you say?' I replied in an upbeat, interested sort of way. Nutters like Bell End like you taking an interest in their mad rants. 'Heck, that is a lot, isn't it, sir?'

'Yes, blast you!' he yelled, fiercely slashing his blade in fury. 'It is impressive. More than impressive, even. Man was a genius! A genius! Eight. Think about it, eh? One, two, three, four, five, six, seven, EIGHT!' He punctuated each number with a forward lunge – each looked pretty similar to me.

'Oh,' I said quietly. 'So he was quite, erm, prolific, then?' I added, showing him I was all ears and keen as mustard on this Jerzy chap.

Bell End glared at me and pressed the point of his sabre into the floor to flex it. I began to feel afraid.

'Sabre is like poker –' he started, but like the mad blurter I am, I interjected.

'Professor Sullivan said it was a physical game of chess.'

'I'm talking about *bluff*, girl. Bluff. Bluff, damn you! Go on, say the word!'

I looked at Portia and Portia looked at me, and we both knew what had to be done. 'Erm, bluff, sir,' we muttered.

This seemed to pacify him, though. He began to speak to us more gently. 'You're both excellent bloody fencers.

Excellent for interschool matches, that is, but you're playing tournament now.' And then he started yelling again. 'Tournament! Do you *really* know what that means? It's not like a cosy friendly between schools with cheerful salutes and etiquette, followed by finger sandwiches and tea.'

I didn't interrupt, but in all my time at interschool fencing matches I'd never been offered a single finger sandwich. A glass of juice and some crisps were as good as it ever got.

Bell End was on a roll, though. 'No, you've got tantrums, threats, bullying, and more important, the bloody-minded focus of girls who have been waiting their whole life to rip you to shreds and dance on your entrails. And on top of that you've got all those scouts and FIE spies, wandering about, lurking, spooking. Then, of course, there's the fan clubs.'

'Fan clubs?' I blurted as an image of cheerleaders like we have in the States popped into my mind. Pom-poms being waved and cheers of support as they cried:

'Give me C!' *'C!'*
'Give me an A!' *'A!'*
'Give me an L!' *'L!'*
'Give me a Y!' *'Y!'*
'Give me a P!' *'P!'*
'Give me an S!' *'S!'*
'Give me an O!' *'O!'*
'What does it spell?'
'CALYPSO! Yaaaaah!'
It seemed very unlikely in England.

'You mean fans for the fencers, Mr Wellend?' Because however unlikely cheerleaders might be, I was quite excited about the idea of a fan club. I'd never imagined fencers to have fan clubs. I know polo players and footballers have them, but fencing had always seemed to me like the chess club of sports. I wondered if they'd write me fan letters.

But Bell End brought me crashing back down to reality with a thud. 'Yes, fan clubs. I'm not talking about girls like *you*, but mark my words: weak, gutless fencers get their families and friends to come to cheer them on in the hope of intimidating their opponents.'

'Oh my God!' I cried, suddenly envisioning Sarah running up and down the piste crying out, 'Go Boojie! Go Boojie!'

'And presumably you both have aspirations for the National Team, and to make that you've got to place third at the very least. The very least. And let me pop another of your girlish little dream bubbles. All the competitors you'll be up against are going to be as good as, if not better than, you.'

I was a bit insulted by that girlish-little-dream-bubble remark and almost blurted an objection, but Portia nudged me.

'And make no mistake, it is in my interest as much as yours that you succeed in your goals to make it to the Nationals. When I take you up to Sheffield on Saturday, all the other masters will be looking at *me*, yes, *me*. They'll be looking to see what I've done with you. How well I've whipped you into shape and trained you up. And I don't want to be a laughing stock. Which is why I'll be teaching you on a one-to-one every day on top of your regular classes.'

'Thank you, Bell End, I mean Mr Wellend,' I said quickly.

'And I've got another surprise for you too, girlies.'

Something about the glint in his eye made me suspect it wasn't going to be a nice surprise – like a finger sandwich, for example.

'I'll be using two sabres to fence you!'

'Sir?' Portia questioned.

'One in each hand. Double the challenge, double the lesson. We can't afford to waste time, Briggs. Now grab your weapon, you're up first. Kelly, wire her up.'

I did as I was told, as Bell End grabbed another sabre off the wall of the salle and wired himself up. Then I sat on the bench for what would be the most incredible lesson in sabre tactics I had ever witnessed.

Bell End was shorter than Portia, but with the two sabres in his hand he cut an imposing, if not terrifying, figure. Sort of like the Incredible Hulk with elegance. His gruff ways off the piste didn't match the grace and speed he displayed thereon. He was lightning-fast and had the supreme footwork of a dancer. As much as I love taking the piss out of poor old Bell End, I had to admit I was spellbound.

I watched Portia too as she was forced to fence on a different level than I'd seen her fence before. She advanced and retreated with such control that her torso didn't even seem to be moving, and the speed of her sword and Bell End's two weapons was so fast, I didn't know what was going on. The buzzers and lights of the recording box just kept buzzing and flashing.

After their bout, Portia took her mask off and shook out her hair. Instead of her usual perfect hair-commercial coif, which I had always been so envious of, a spray of sweat such as I'd never seen shot out of her hair for a metre or more.

'See what I mean, Briggs? You were forced to up your game. Well done. Now, Kelly, git up here. Briggs, wire her up.'

Having had the advantage of watching Portia, I knew what I was in for. With two blades coming at me simultaneously, I realised how lethal the combination of wrist action, speed and surprise can be. What really struck me, though, was the simplicity of Bell End's actions. For the first time in my fencing life, I could see the vital importance of drawing my opponent with bluffs. Of course I'd bluffed before – it's the nature of the game – but with two sabres coming at me I had to let go of preplanned strategies and trust my instinct.

I took a lot of hits, but I struck a few of my own as well and, when we took our masks off, Bell End did the most extraordinary thing. He bowed. Yes, he bowed at *me*, Calypso Kelly, and it was a low, graceful, princely bow too.

Portia was clapping.

'Miss Kelly, I honour you. You're a bloody fine little fencer, girl, and you'll see the Olympics if I have any control over it, mark my words. And we men from Capers don't make idle threats.'

I was wet with sweat and slightly dazed by exhaustion and what Bell End had just told me. In the next minute Portia swept me up in a hug and spun me around. 'Do you know how amazing you are?' she asked, laughing.

'I only know *something* amazing has just happened,' I told her, laughing in what I believe is termed a giddy way.

Neither Portia nor I could come down to earth after what had happened. The rest of the day's lessons passed in a blur. I was probably going to fail all my GCSEs, but I felt like I'd taken a leap into another part of my body and my life. I felt that new vistas awaited me, new exhilarating possibilities were beckoning. I was texting under my desk throughout every lesson.

MAD, MAD, MAD, FANTASTIC FENCING CLASS TODAY. WILL TELL ALL LATER. ARE YOU GOING TO SHEFFIELD SATURDAY? PLEASE SAY YES XXXXXXX C

(For once I was too exhilarated to hold back on my kisses and just pressed 'Send'.)

NO! 2 BUSY HANGING OUT WITH U IN WINDSOR REMEMBER! FREDS XX

Whoops!

ACTUALLY, I AM GOING TO THE FENCING TOURNAMENT IN SHEFFIELD, THOUGHT YOU WOULD BE TOO? X CALYPSO

(I limited myself to one kiss to make up for my earlier effusiveness.)

NO, JUST DOING THE REGIONALS AND NATIONALS. BUT GOOD LUCK. LET'S MAKE IT SUNDAY, OK? FREDS XXX

DEAL! XXX CALYPSO

Did I mention that I have the most understanding and wise boyfriend in *all* of Christendom and beyond? Well, I have. My spirits soared once more. Even when Honey started making some poisonous jibe about my plebeian mother and Clapham, I riposted with a pretty sharp comeback of my own. 'Oh, bugger off, Honey.'

Sadly, Sarah was neither as wise nor as understanding as my boyfriend. She called me soon after and rattled on for what seemed like forever about how she was going to pick me up after classes on Saturday and take me back to London to see the house in Clapham. 'Oh, Mumsy can't wait for her Boojems to see the house.'

'But Mumsy, I mean, Sarah, there's a really important fencing tournament in Sheffield on Saturday, which means we'll be heading off at six in the morning and won't be back until the evening. So you see –'

'Oh, wonderful. I'll come and watch.'

Again I felt horrible as I lied – but I still did. 'That would be great, but the thing is they don't let observers come. It's a real shame. I was really looking forward to seeing the house.'

'No, no, no, of course it's more important that you attend this tournament. You know how much I support your fencing. Never mind. I'll pick you up Sunday, darling. We'll have a . . .'

I didn't listen to the rest of her baby-talk babblings. I was just too wildly depressed. I mean I love Sarah and I wanted to support her over her midlife crisis with Bob but, well, I was soooo looking forward to seeing Freddie on Sunday that . . . oh, I don't know, it was all a mess!

When I told my friends about my dilemma over brown slops in the refectory at dinner, though, Star said, 'Just explain to Sarah you're meeting Freddie on Sunday. Parents hate thinking they're inhibiting your social life.'

'Exactly, darling,' Indie agreed. 'All 'rents are terrified that if they get in the way of your social life, you'll become a friendless nobody.'

Everyone nodded knowingly.

'Just explain about how exhausted you'll be from the tournament and suggest lunch in Windsor instead. After lunch, simply say you've got to meet up with your boyfriend. She'll understand,' Indie naively reasoned.

If I knew Sarah as well as I thought I did – though lately she'd been rather odd – it would take more than straitjackets, armed police and attack dogs to prevent Sarah from meeting Freddie. You see, in my friends' privileged world of Daddy's plastic and Mummy's contacts, freedom, like status, was taken for granted. And it was no use trying to explain to my friends that Sarah would see it as a mother's duty to meet her daughter's first boyfriend. And that's without even taking into account that he was heir to the throne of Britain. No, Sarah would want to interview him and take photographs and everything.

As I looked around at my friends' supportive faces, I knew they could never comprehend that Sarah might not be convinced to blithely say ta-ta and wave me off to meet up with my boyfriend. My friends' parents would be mortified at the prospect of being seen as interfering or overprotective.

Of course they want their children to be safe and well, but they figure by age four any intelligent child (and of course with their genes their children are all wildly intelligent – NOT) can sort out their own social lives. They had been serving alcohol at meals to their children since they were out of their high chairs and all thought it perfectly natural for them to help themselves to the cocktail shaker when at home. If you treat your children like civilised adults, they'll behave like civilised adults, went the philosophy. I was on the wrong side of a cultural barrier that would take a lifetime to explain. So I didn't even try.

Indie called one of her bodyguards over and as I observed him do his duty, piling the remainder of Indie's brown slops into the pocket of his jacket, I suddenly thought, what if Sarah called me Boojie in front of Freds? *Quelle horreur!*

Everyone knows that princes are renowned for their understanding and wisdom, but still, even princes must have their limits.

FIVE

My Knickers Were in a Right Twist

Later in the afternoon, I received an e-mail from Sarah which sent my spirits plummeting like a dead dove to the ground.

My Darling Boojiem [what was it with this constant use of her old baby name for me?]
I have arranged with Sister Constance to take you out on Sunday after Mass as we discussed. Just the two of us, won't that be super?
Love,
Mumsy xxxxx

My knickers were in a right twist now! The situation was far, far graver than I had first thought — and that was pretty grave indeed. My mother was regressing, or was it reverting? I'd read about this reverting business in the *Dummy's Guide to Psycho Babble* only recently. According to the book, baby-talk in adults is the final stage before dribbling, incontinence and compulsive thumb-sucking set in. Any idea I had entertained about explaining my parents' split to Freds were splattered like road kill now.

And then I realised that *Gladesdale* would hardly be thrilled about having a dribbling, nappy-wearing, baby-talker on their writing team, however lowbrow their show might be.

Ipso facto, the wise men and women of *Gladesdale* might well give Sarah her marching orders – or at least call for a pram to take her away. And as Bob earned, let me see, about, oh, nada, this would mean Sarah couldn't pay my school fees. Had this been the case even a year ago, I would have worn bells on my ankles and bounced about like a folk dancer at a village fair. But now it was an entirely different story. I adored Saint Augustine's, I adored my friends. I adored my life – even with my nemesis Honey plonked right in the middle of it.

I had to take decisive action. There would be no more messing about or talk of 'creative endeavours'. Bob would simply have to give up the madness of his Big One and take Sarah back to LA for clinical treatment. Preferably before Sunday.

Dear Daddy, [I wasn't going to 'Bob' him any more. He needed to be reminded of his parental and husbandly duties.]
The situation is far graver than I first led you to believe. Come IMMEDIATELY, before *Gladesdale* calls for a pram to take Mummy off to the loony asylum for reverting. She's not quite in diapers yet, but it's only a matter of time, and then who

will pay my fees? I'll have to go to one of those Hollywood schools you've always hated so much. No, dearest padre, now is not the time for creative endeavours. Your wife is on the verge of requiring potty training and your daughter will be school-less! Tell me your flight times.

Your loving daughter,

Calypso

PS: Please make sure you come BEFORE SUNDAY! URGENT! BEFORE SUNDAY!

As always, he must have been at his laptop because he fired off his response with lightning speed.

Dearest Daughter, ['Daughter' indeed, how droll! Well if he thought drollness would make things right, he was very much mistaken.]

You have begged me for years to go to a 'normal school'. Consider this your Big Break. Besides, I love and trust Sarah enough to know that you are exaggerating her mental state. You weren't awarded the title Queen of the Doomsday Prophecies for nothing. I am working night and day to get this script finished so that I can give Sarah (and you) the lives you both deserve. I haven't slept since Sarah left, and a bit of support from my own daughter would be much appreciated. In the meantime, enjoy your mother's company and stop whining.

Your loving father,

Bob xxx

PS: It is ALWAYS the time for creative endeavors, Calypso! You of all people should know that.

If it wasn't a sin to dishonour your parents, I would have told him to bugger off and boil his head in his Big One. Instead I held fire and shared my despair with Portia, Georgina, Indie, Clemmie, Arabella and Star over a pile of tuck and a sip or two from our Body Shop Specials. Honey was there too, stretched out like a lioness on her bed, but I had reached the stage with Honey where I was pretty much able to pretend that she didn't exist.

'I feel soooo disloyal about Sarah. I mean, I know she's distressed and upset and I *do* want to see her Sunday, I *do*! But I want to see Freddie as well and, believe me, I know my mad madre will not just say ta-ta and wave me off. It's not the American way,' I explained as I took a sip of the vodka that Star passed me.

'Darling, you could always combine the two,' Star suggested. 'I'm sure Freddie would *love* to meet Sarah. I think she's cool. Totally bonkers obviously, but cool.'

'Well, yes, but –'

'Though Calypso can hardly pull Freds with Sarah looking on,' Georgina reminded her. Finally, some sanity from my posse!

I didn't say anything, but the last thing I wanted was my baby-talking, reverting mother scaring Freds off. Is that evil? I think it probably is.

'What about the plan for the two of you to have a lovely mother-daughter lunch somewhere fabulous in Windsor and ducking off to meet Freddie afterwards?' asked Indie.

'But you don't understand. Sarah will want to come,' I insisted.

'Not if you suggest to Sarah that she might like to meet him on another more formal occasion, like a proper lunch the next weekend? Apart from anything else, she might be feeling a bit stronger by then,' Portia suggested as she unwound the towel turban her hair had been drying in. Her idea was pure genius. I wanted to hug her but settled for passing her the vodka.

'Brilliant,' George agreed. ''Rents love it when you suggest things they think they'll have to force you to do.'

'Is Boojie-Woojie ashamed of her mumsy, then?' asked Honey in a baby-voice.

I threw a Jelly Baby at her but unfortunately she caught it adroitly on her serpent-like tongue. 'And I thought you PC Americans were soooo keen on the Christian values of honouring your folks?' She said all this in a bad attempt at a piss-take of a southern accent. I think it is the only American accent she knows how to do.

'Oh, and what might we have here?' demanded Miss Bibsmore, suddenly appearing in our doorway.

All of us sat there on the floor looking dumbstruck. None of us had heard her stick coming down the corridor, and as I looked down, I saw why. She'd wrapped a square of carpet to the bottom of her stick in duct tape.

'Just a little chat, Miss Bibsmore. Would you like a sweet?' Portia asked casually, offering up a bag of marsh-mallows.

'No, I would not like a sweet, thank you, Briggsie, but I would like to smell what it is you've been drinking from that shampoo bottle.'

You could hear the collective gulp of our room as Star passed up the Body Shop bottle to Miss Bibsmore.

Miss Bibsmore sniffed it, wrinkled her nose and then stuffed one of her stumpy old fingers in it. Licking her finger, she pronounced, 'Vodka.'

'Yes, it's a special, erm, shampoo they're doing this season, Miss Bibsmore,' I blurted. 'It makes your hair wildly glossy and, well, lovely and soft. Portia's just used some on her hair . . .' I pointed to Portia's lovely, freshly-washed, glossy hair.

Miss Bibsmore ignored my mad rant. 'I'll hazard it's yours, Miss O'Hare,' she said, turning her attention to Honey.

'You'll hazard no such thing, you mad, old witch. Why would it be mine?'

'Oh, I've got my eye on you, madam.'

'A blind eye, maybe,' Honey sneered, her collagen-pumped lips blistering with derision.

'Well, evidence would suggest that, as I don't see young Mr Tobias in the room, you are the most likely suspect an' all.'

'What's Tobias got to do with it? He's a soft toy!' Honey argued, bug-eyed with the horror that she was being so unfairly persecuted. In Honey's mind, she had the patent on unfair persecution. I almost felt a bit sorry for her, although she was only making matters worse for herself by referring to Tobias as a 'soft toy'. I mean, we are talking about a bear with his own custom-made LVT trunk and designer outfits.

'How dare you!' Georgina spat, diving off the floor and looming over Honey's bed, her eyes flashing with fury.

Miss Bibsmore interjected, placing her stick between Georgina and Honey. 'Soft toy or no, he's a full fee-paying student at this school and the only other student, apart from you, Miss O'Hare, in my dormitory what 'as a drinking problem.'

'Tobias has given up drinking,' Georgina assured Miss Bibsmore earnestly. 'He took himself off to detox over half-term.'

Miss Bibsmore thought about this and nodded. 'Well, I hope the treatment sticks an' all, Miss Castle Orpington, and that's genuine, that is. But Mr Tobias isn't my concern on this occasion. So, Miss O'Hare, you can come down with me to Sister Constance.'

'This is outrageous. You have singled me out for persecution since you first laid eyes on me.'

I could relate to that, as that was exactly what Honey had done to me.

Miss Bibsmore cackled. 'Well, you were the one wot told me that you sued the last person what treated you like everyone else.'

'Ugh!' Honey grunted as she started punching numbers into her phone. 'Well, I'm calling my lawyers! There are witnesses here who have just heard you admit you're singling me out −'

Miss Bibsmore swooped on the little gem-like phone and pocketed it. 'You can call your lawyers after you've spoken to Sister. Now up you get, one, two, three.'

The rest of us sat in stunned silence as Miss Bibsmore bustled the loudly protesting Honey from the room. We waited all of a minute before bursting into raucous laughter.

The maddest thing was that we still had the rest of our Body Shop Specials piled amongst our tuck feast.

SIX

Be Warned! Life's NOT All Nicey-Nicey

Naturally, I couldn't follow the advice of my friends to overlap my meeting with Sarah with my meeting with Freddie. After careful thought I decided even Portia's flawless plan left room for random 'rental disobedience. I knew how much Sarah was longing to meet Freds. Formal lunches sounded all well and good, but formality and Sarah were just not a natural fit. I had no choice. Imagine Freds, heir to the throne, meeting my baby-talking-reverting mother? He'd run a mile – with Sarah following him in hot pursuit.

No, as dismal a prospect as it was, I would have to put Sarah first and cancel Freds. I tried and tried to think of an alternative, but I owed it to Sarah to be there for her in her time of need. There was no way out. As I composed the text the next evening, little tears banked up behind my eyes at the thought that I wasn't going to see Freds on Sunday and feel his lovely lips on mine, or smell the lovely lemony smell of his neck.

SOZ, BUT SUNDAY ISN'T GO TO WORK, THE MADRE'S IN TOWN AND WANTS ME ALL TO HERSELF. NEXT SATURDAY, THOUGH, PROMISE. XXXX CALYPSO

I watched the screen of my mobile for what seemed like an eternity, but there was no response, and eventually I had to go off to study period. I told myself that he was obviously wildly busy . . . either that or furious and planning to dump me.

By Saturday morning at five a.m., when my alarm woke us for our drive up to the tournament in Sheffield, Freds *still* hadn't responded to my texts. Yes, tragic as it sounds, I'd sent several texts because each time I told myself he was probably in divs (that's what they call lessons at Eades) or chapel, or well, just very, very busy loading up his iPod. After my recent phone text face-off with Freddie before half-term – which turned out to be all Honey's fault – I wasn't going to let any sort of misunderstanding between us happen again.

After Freds' reaction to Honey selling that mobile phone snap to the tabloids, Star has always thought Freddie was overly keen on himself. She's always telling me I'm too good for him, but then she's so fiercely loyal she doesn't think any boy is good enough for me. I hadn't told Star that I had chucked meeting Freds on Sunday altogether because I didn't want him to meet my regressing madre. She would not have been impressed by that, nor, deep down, was I, but . . . well, I could hardly have Sarah baby-talking to the heir to the throne, could I? In the past three days she'd called me diddums, like, nine times! Diddums? What was I, a cat?

On Saturday morning, Portia and I dressed in our jeans and hoodies in the en suite so as not to wake Honey, who was snoring so loudly, I swear, it's a miracle she didn't wake herself up. Then we rushed down the stairs with our torches and out across the damp lawn to Saint Theresa's convent, where the tiny little form of Sister Regina was already at the door waiting for us in an overexcited state. She was hopping from one foot to the other.

It had been decided by Sister Constance that one of the nuns should chaperone us to the tournament, and so they'd played poker and the lucky winner was Sister Regina. After a lot of nun-ish clucking and cuddling and telling us how all the other nuns were sick with jealously, she led us into the kitchen of the convent, which hadn't been updated since the fifties.

She'd cooked us a full English breakfast, bless her. 'Well, you'll need the nutrition with all that swordplay you'll be doing. And I've packed tuna sandwiches for the journey!'

'Oh, that's really sweet, Sister,' Portia and I told her.

'Only, don't say a word to Sister Michael, because it was her tin of tuna I used.'

'Sister!' we chastised.

'Oh, stop. We each get a little treat in the weekly shop, see, only I always choose cigarettes,' she explained, dropping her voice to a low whisper.

'Sister, that's very, very naughty. Now we'll feel guilty,' Portia teased. 'Poor Sister Michael.'

'Oh, shush,' she said, cackling wickedly as she bustled

busily about the kitchen, dishing out the eggs, bacon, sausages, toast and baked beans on to the old, chipped green plates. 'Sister Michael won't even remember she ordered it. She's about to reach her century in another month, she is.'

'Wow!' I exclaimed. 'That's . . . totally cool.'

'Yes, and they'll be a big tea with scones and cream not to mention cucumber *and* tuna sandwiches. We're all looking forward to it, but while the body may be strong, the mind's not all it could be in Sister Michael's case, bless her. Last night when we were playing animal snap, she didn't get *one* hand in. Even the chicken had her flummoxed and she always gets the chicken – always. Anyway, she wouldn't mind. Truth is, all of us nuns are very proud of you, and I'm sure no one could begrudge two lovely girls like you a little tuna. Now eat up and stop fussing.'

We were just scraping our plates when we heard Bell End knocking on the door of the convent. It was only six o'clock now and still dark, so all four of us used our torches to make our way to the school mini-bus. Bell End gallantly led Sister Regina through the wet grass. 'Isn't this exciting, girls?' she kept exclaiming. 'Oh, Mr Wellend, I do hope they do well.'

Bell End had already packed our kit. 'Can't trust you bloody girls to remember your own heads,' he'd insisted when we'd offered to help the day before. 'No, leave it to the master; at least that way I'll know everything's in order.'

Sister Regina sat up front with Bell End and took control of the radio, which she set to Radio One and started singing along to an old Britney Spears song. When I say singing along, I mean 'nun-singing', because obviously she didn't get to hear that many pop songs in the convent, so she just sang 'la-la-la-diddlie-dah' to the tune.

Bell End had brought along a few cushions to prop her up on, so she could see over the dashboard. Portia nudged me, 'Do you think he might be a big softy after all?' she whispered.

'No!' I told her firmly, rubbing my arm, which was still bruised from the training session the day before with our two-sabre-wielding maniac of a fencing master.

Most of the journey, Bell End prepared us for what awaited us at the other end. 'It's not all nicey-nicey like interschool. You've got to expect all sorts. You've got those that play dirty and those that play clean in a nasty sort of way. Just like in poker, they'll use anything but skill to bluff or intimidate as they see fit. And another thing, you've got to ignore the Great Badger Rapists.'

'Sir?' I asked.

'Them prats with GBR written on their backs.'

'But why?' I asked, because, truly, that was all I dreamed of, being one of those prats with KELLY GBR (Great Britain) emblazoned across *my* back.

'Because you only get that honour if you've made the National Squad and are fencing internationally,' explained Bell End. 'Only there are some that award themselves the honour. I keep telling you, fencing's not all nicey-nicey.'

'But that's cheating!' I cried out indignantly over the top of Sister Regina's la-la-diddlie-dahing.

'Pathetic, that's what it is. These prats get themselves colours made up for tournament intimidation. They figure it'll scare the bejesus out of you.'

'How elaborate,' Portia remarked. 'Elaborate' was Portia's ultimate toff put-down. By elaborate she meant, scheming, low-life, social-climbing pond scum.

'That's one word for it, Briggs.' Bell End chuckled. I think he was starting to pick up on Portia's aristocratic codes, Mistress of the Understatement that she was.

'Then, of course, they'll have their fan clubs, you know, family, friends and the like. Mates from school, anyone they can dig up. Some of them even pay groupies to cheer them on. Even the bravest sabreur can be thrown when their opponent's end of the piste is full of a cheering squad yelling for blood, and your end's empty,' he said as if speaking from personal experience. 'You girls will be all right today with Sister here and me, but there will be times when the lonely fear hits you, when you don't even have someone to plug in your body wire and they've got people chanting, 'Cut the guts out of the South African wanker!' Only being South African, he pronounced it *winker*.

Luckily Sister was loudly diddle-dee-deeing to a song, so she didn't hear the profanity. Portia and I looked at one another. Clearly Bell End had had some painful personal experience in this area.

He elaborated a bit more about the abuse we could expect. Portia and I both sneered though at the thought of such obvious and puerile intimidation tactics. Star and the others had *begged* to come and watch us, but we agreed that we'd be too stressed out and that, if anything, it might put us off.

'So, you've got to shut down emotionally. Understood? Think with your brain, move with your body, slam 'em with your blade,' Bell End insisted. 'That's your business. Your *only* business. The rest of the carry-on, the taunting of the opponent's fans, the verbal abuse they'll sling at you – none of that matters. Just GFTB, git it? Go for the Bollocks! Let that be your battle cry.'

Since Bell End's arrival at Saint Augustine's, GFTB had slipped into our everyday speech. Portia and I often giggled when Bell End shouted it out at us when it was just the two of us fencing. For a start, as girls, we didn't have bollocks. Also, I don't think Sister Constance or our parents would appreciate our young minds being exposed to such obscenities. We, after all, were the crème de la crème of teenage girls.

Sister Regina, who'd happily been la-la-la-diddlie-dahing to a heavy rap song, actually heard this and was horrified. 'Oooh, Mr Wellend, language.' This seemed odd as the song Sister had been nun-singing along to was positively littered with obscenities, all of which celebrated the joys of sinning.

'Sorry, Sister,' he apologised, his face glowing red with embarrassment.

'And don't forget, girls,' Sister shouted out over another filthy rap song about gunning down rivals, 'I'll be there, praying for you. A decade of the rosary is worth a thousand fan clubs. All this artifice that Mr Wellend has warned you about will melt away under the divine intervention of Our Lady, girls. *Always* remember that.'

'Yes, Sister,' we agreed.

'And if they get too crude, I shall wave my rosary at them in defiance, I will.'

'That should have them trembling in their boots,' Bell End muttered under his breath.

'But honestly, Mr Wellend, I hope you won't mind if I call out a little *hoorah!* now and then if the girls get a particularly good goal or such like?'

Bless. I could have reached over and cuddled her. Nuns are so sweetly unworldly.

'No, I'm sure that would be most appropriate, Sister . . .' I think even Bell End was a bit choked up by her innocence.

'Good, because I do like a nice little cheer, Mr Wellend. Revs up the engines, it does.'

We made good time and arrived at the BFA Sheffield Open venue a little earlier than planned. But there were already dozens of other vehicles there; some of them like ours, with their school motifs on them, others just random cars and mini-buses, which had presumably transported the dreaded fan clubs. Bell End pointed out that most people would have come by train. That meant there was going to be a *lot* of people at the tournament. I think that's when it really hit me just how defining an event this was going to be in my fencing career.

Portia and I pulled our heavy kits out of the mini-bus while Bell End lifted our little nun out of the car. At four foot nothing, she was like a doll. One that was becoming increasingly wound up with excitement!

And that was when all Bell End's pep talks turned into a worthless heap of rubbish. Because that was when I heard the word 'Boojie!' as my mother appeared out of nowhere, just as we entered the building. 'Isn't this exciting? Oh, let me look at you,' she cried, grabbing my cheeks and pinching them. 'You'll knock them dead!' She was incandescent with pride.

I, on the other hand, was incandescent with quite another emotion altogether.

SEVEN

My Tragic Fan Club

It was difficult to make it even to the table near the entrance, where we had to have our names ticked off for the pools. Apart from the crowds, Sarah was wrapped around my body like a limpet, and Sister Regina was hanging off my fencing kit, chirping, 'Just wait till I tell all the other nuns about this. I know it's sinful, but I'll revel in their envy, I will.'

Portia managed to have her name ticked off and made her way imperiously through the throngs of people, many of whom we'd soon be slamming with our blades. Everyone was just mingling and chatting amicably, which made me doubt Bell End's fearsome stories of what we'd be up against, although I did see a few fencers with GBR on their backs wandering about the hall. Bell End nudged me. 'See what I mean? GBR my arse, they're Great Badger Rapists, you mark my words. But they think if you see that you'll be intimidated.'

'Pathetic,' I agreed, as I finally made it to the desk, weighed down with the twin burden of my mother and my dread of what she might do to embarrass me. Bell End slapped my back. I think he was being supportive but, unaware of his own strength, he winded me, and I fell on to the book with all the names written on it.

'Christ Almighty, look what we've got here,' some Hoorah Henry joked to his mateage, and they all laughed loudly.

'Don't you get cheeky, gentlemen, or I'll have your master on to you, I will,' Sister Regina threatened, raising herself up to her full four feet. Nuns can be surprisingly imperious and menacing, especially where boys are concerned. They reddened at her threat and muttered, 'Sorry, Sister.'

Any menace her threat may have held, however, was immediately dissolved by Sarah, who threw her arms around me and told them to leave me alone. 'Big bullies!'

I unwound her arms from around my neck and looked her in the eye. 'Look, Sarah, seriously, you can't do that here. I'm not five any more.'

'You'll always be my little, widdle girl, Calypso,' she promised me with another cheek pinch – as if this might actually cheer me up.

After finally having my name ticked off, I chased after Portia, who was already nearing the changing rooms.

'See you later, widdle, widdle girl,' the Hoorah Henrys called after me.

Sarah, who was tagging along, didn't say anything, but I think she realised she'd landed me in it.

It was all I could do to shake her off at the changing rooms. Fortunately, Sister Regina had already been seduced by the tea table. If you ever wanted to kidnap a nun, all you'd have to do is to offer them a nice cup of tea and they'd go anywhere.

'You sure you don't want me to help you change into your fencing outfit, darling?' Sarah asked at the changing rooms.

I shut the door on her with a firm 'No, thank you'.

'I take it you weren't expecting Sarah?' Portia put it to me. She didn't look too happy about it, either.

'Of course not. I told her they didn't allow non-fencers, but, well, she's lived in America for a long time. Mothers sort of learn how to push pretty hard over there, you see.'

'I know it sounds horrible, but I am sooo glad we didn't bring a fan club. I would be ten times more nervous with Star and the others watching us.'

I agreed.

There was a crowd of other girls kitting up, so we let the conversation drop. No one spoke to us, and we didn't attempt to speak to them. Portia and I didn't need to say anything to one another, either. It was quite clear that we were both scared out of our wits.

Once we were kitted up we wandered back out into the maelstrom of the hall, which had twice the number of people crowded into it compared to when we'd first arrived.

We couldn't see Bell End, although I spotted Sarah chatting to Sister Regina by the tea table. Portia and I looked about to see what we should be doing, but everything was utter chaos. There were loads of random announcements coming over the loudspeaker, which further added to the confusion.

'If there are any qualified presidents in the hall today who have not volunteered, could they please come forward, as we are short of referees today,' bellowed the loudspeaker.

Bell End suddenly appeared out of nowhere and sprinted swiftly towards the other end of the hall like he was about to receive another Olympic medal. Sister Regina started to clap and cheer him on. Sarah, looking a little dazed, joined her.

'Let's do some stretches,' I suggested to Portia in the hope that in doing a few low lunges, Sarah wouldn't be able to spot us.

'Can Simon Tyler please report to sign in, as you have not yet registered?' blared a voice over the loudspeaker.

'Everything seems so disorganised,' Portia remarked as people stepped over us. 'I don't have a clue what we're meant to be doing. There's no boards about pools or where we're meant to be fencing, nothing.'

'Attention!' the announcer called over the loudspeaker. 'The girls' pools will be starting shortly. And I repeat, Simon Tyler, report to registration, NOW!' Then the names for the girls' pools were rattled off.

'This is it,' I said to Portia as several names were called and asked to assemble at piste five. Portia's name came up in the next lot of pools being held on piste six. My name was called to the pools being held at piste seven.

'Well, should we shake hands or something, do you think?' I blurted in that special idiotic way I have.

I was feeling the adrenaline begin to course through my veins as the calls for Simon Tyler to come to registration became increasingly threatening.

'No, I think we should hug,' Portia insisted. And so we did.

Of course, my mother and Sister Regina had also heard our names called and were waiting for me at piste seven with a banner they'd cobbled together out of a stolen table-cloth. They were clutching it with the pride of two women who've just knitted a quilt.

It read – and this causes me some agony to relay – *Go Boojie! Go!* The words were written in jam.

And then out of the blue I wished Bob were here. He'd know just what to say – even if it was one of his stupid foot-ball chants from his college years. Also, Bob actually did know quite a bit about fencing, whereas Sarah's support was purely emotional.

The other girls assembled at my piste began to giggle as I approached and Sarah and Sister Regina began to chant, 'Go Boojie! Go!' Unfortunately, I don't think anyone was in any doubt as to who Boojie was.

Bell End strode over to our piste in a very authoritative manner with a referee's clipboard. As he was to preside over our bouts, he didn't make eye contact with me.

He had an officious air about him as he said, 'Right, first up, Kelly and Rogers-Staughten-Bowhip. And ladies,' he added, looking over at Sister and Sarah sternly, 'I think we can dispense with the banner for the pools.'

'Boooooh!' Sarah called out. 'Spoilsport!'

It was conflicting on so many levels. Part of me was relieved and the other part felt sorry for the sweet effort Sister and Sarah had put into their banner, even if it was a banner of shame. Also, I just knew that if Bob were here he would have stuck up for their right to express themselves.

Rogers-Staughten-bloody-Bowhip wasn't conflicted, though. She was in spasms of laughter as she shook my hand. But then another random girl hooked me up from the back, which made me feel like maybe I wasn't the total object of ridicule I imagined.

Rogers-Staughten-Bowhip was practically choking on her own mirth during the salute, and I caught a look in Bell End's eye. It was just a glance, but he seemed to be reminding me of what I was there for. If Rogers-Staughten-Bowhip thought she could intimidate me over a banner crafted in jam by a four foot nun and a regressing runaway mother, she was about to discover that she was very much mistaken.

From the moment 'play' was called, I could already taste victory. 'You are Jerzy Pawlowski,' I told myself. Rogers-Staughten-Bowhip's ridicule was to cost her dearly, because all my emotions fell away. As I advanced down the piste, I was thinking with my head, moving with my body and, within seconds, slamming her with my blade. I took all five points and the game was mine.

It had been a ridiculously easy victory, but I wasn't kidding myself that the day was mine. We hadn't even started the direct elimination, which was where things would get ugly.

But Sarah and Sister were thrilled and tried to pick me

up and carry me on their shoulders, a manoeuvre that all went horribly wrong as I became entangled in my own body wire.

'Git off the bloody piste, yer idiots!' Bell End yelled, and they dropped me on their banner, leaving me smeared in jam.

Over at the tea table, I bumped into Billy.

'Bit of a bloody one, I see?' he teased, pointing at the jam on my *lamé*.

'Oh yaah, killer of a match.' I shrugged, in a faux boast.

'But you triumphed?'

'You should see my opponent.'

'You pulped her?'

'And then some.'

Billy laughed, but our lovely banter was halted by Rogers-Staughten-Bowhip, who clearly hadn't been humbled enough en piste because she sidled up and said, 'Good game, *Boojie*.' The derisive emphasis she put on the word 'Boojie' made me want to kick her.

'Boojie?' Billy repeated, looking understandably confused.

'Don't ask,' I replied. 'All you need to know is that it involves a nun, a regressing mother and my opponent here, a wannabe that isn't.' Then I stormed off because I could see Sarah and Sister Regina coming towards me.

Back in the changing rooms, I wiped the jam off and checked my mobile, still vainly hoping that Freddie might ultimately forgive me for chucking him two dates running. I didn't really think he would, but I needed a sign from God at this point that all was not lost. And there it was.

SOZ ABOUT BEING A DICK AND NOT TEXTING BEFORE NOW.
THINKING OF YOU, MISSING YOU. CALL ME WHEN YOU'RE DONE
RINSING THEM ALL, FREDS XXX

EIGHT

She Who
Would Valiant Be

I t turned out that Bell End wasn't exaggerating about the intimidation and cheap-trick tactics of tournaments. I had made it through four gruelling rounds of direct elimination, and now I was at the finals.

Yes, the finals. Now it was just down to me and Jenny Frogmorten. Freddie's text had given me all the confidence I needed to play my best. Also, Bell End's pep talk *had* actually helped me keep my focus as my opponent's fan club did everything they could to humiliate and undermine me. As I was being wired up they were already calling me an 'F-ing sad case'. It was lucky Bob wasn't here. He'd go ballistic if he heard that sort of language yelled at his daughter.

'Jenny's going to kill you, Kelly!' my opponent's boyfriend yelled while the rest of her fan club hissed.

'Whatever!' I yelled back to show I was bored rather than terrified.

I wasn't fazed. All their taunts couldn't demoralise me, because, apart from getting used to the abuse, I now knew that Freds loved me. Well, he'd sent me a text that was loving. Also, four years of being Honey's torture toy had immunised me to ugly taunts and filthy abuse.

In each bout, I was down my end with Sarah and Sister Regina. And while they may have embarrassed me in the pools with their jam-smeared banner, now I saw no difference in their madness and that of the hordes of filthy-mouthed barbarians up the other end of the piste, cheering on my opponents and abusing me.

In fact I had become rather proud of my posse. Portia had been knocked out in the semi-finals, which still meant she'd placed highly. But while she had been fencing, Sister and Sarah had valiantly run from piste to piste to support each of us through our matches. Now their attention was firmly fixed on *moi*, as was Bell End's, whose presidential duties were done for the day. Portia was over at another end of the hall cheering on Billy as she should, given she was his girlfriend. But still, I missed her, because as this was the last game for the girls that day, my opponent now had practically every other person in the hall backing her. My back-up was very thin, but then they say it's quality not quantity that counts.

'GFTB, Kelly,' Bell End whispered in my ear as he wired me up. 'I'm right here behind you, and I have to warn you, I plan on making a lot of noise.'

'OK,' I replied, figuring he meant cheering.

'Some of what I may yell admittedly isn't fit for poor Sister Regina's ears, but this is war. Git it?'

OK, now I was nervous. 'I'm not sure I understand, Mr Wellend?'

'You don't need to understand, girl. Close your ears to what I yell at them. Your job is to slice that little piece of meat up the other end of the piste to ribbons. So ignore me, it's not for your benefit but for those scum-suckers up there,' he said, indicating the opposing fan club, some of whom were giving me the finger and others who were pep-talking Jenny.

'OK,' I told him. 'So you're going to give as good as we get in terms of abuse?'

'I'm going to give a damn sight better. They're baying for your blood, Kelly, and there are near to a hundred of them. I'm going to bay for Jenny's blood.' Then he pushed me on to the piste.

As I shook my opponent's hand, she leaned in and said, 'Like the banner, Kelly,' only not in a totally unfriendly way.

I probably should explain that said banner *had* deteriorated somewhat during its arduous day. The words now read *Oo Booo Oo*. But Sarah and Sister weren't giving up on it. They clutched both ends of it, jumping up and down with endless energy.

'Thanks,' I said to my opponent. 'So do I; they made it with jam.'

'Jam?' she asked, looking at me as if I were demented.

'It looked better earlier in the day,' I told her, more than happy for her to underestimate me.

The niceties ended there, though. From the moment 'Play' was called, I heard Bell End yelling the abuse he had hinted at earlier. But all the warnings in the world could never have prepared me for, 'Gut the little slag! Gut her like a fish!'

It was hard to ignore, especially with Sarah and Sister singing along to Bell End's chants, converting them all to the tune of 'He Who Would Valiant Be' ('Gut Her! Gut Her! Gut Her Like a Fish!') one of my favourite hymns as it happens – well, at least it *was*.

But I couldn't focus on Bell End or Sister and Sarah's 'hymn'. Jenny was my target. I'd watched her win one of her earlier bouts and I knew she had a penchant for cuts to the wrist and a weakness when it came to defending her mask. It's not unusual, because someone with this preference lets their sword arm hang slightly lower, ready to make their favourite cut.

I therefore resolved to begin my attack in *quinte*. A successful manoeuvre – I won the point – but I knew I couldn't repeat my advantage too frequently or she'd be on to me.

All the while, Bell End was yelling behind me, 'Slice off her ugly head, Kelly, and feed it to the dogs behind her!'

Even the sad cases standing behind my opponent looked shocked by the vitriol of Bell End's verbal abuse, or maybe it was just shock at hearing a sacred hymn profaned by a nun and a reverting mother.

My opponent's fan club's cries of 'Go for her, Jenny!' and 'Go for the kill!' seemed outclassed somehow by Bell End yelling, 'Rip the rodent's throat open and spit down the little hamster's mouth, Kelly.'

After my second point, Jenny's fans upped their ante,

adding a few lame profanities of their own, which sadly lacked any of the originality or imaginative forensic detail of Bell End's.

The first three hits had been mine, but I knew I'd have to diversify my approach if I was to maintain my lead, because Jenny now knew what I knew. Sure enough, she scored the next hit on my mask after perfectly riposting my attack to *quinte*.

She was fast and she was smart. That's why she'd made it to the finals.

Somewhere in the background I could hear Bell End up his ante in a vitriolic personal attack on the remainder of Jenny's fan club, detailing what he was going to do to them after the competition and mentioning he had ways of finding out where they lived and finding their loved ones, whom he planned to mete out similar vengeful bloody justice to.

'And mete out vengeful justice,' sang Sister and Sarah sweetly to the tune of a hymn I would never be able to sing with the same sense of piety again.

The stream of abuse carried me through to match point fourteen, which meant everything hinged on the final point. Bell End fell silent, although Sister and Sarah valiantly kept up their Pilgrim's Progress of Filth, undeterred by the yellow card the president had threatened them with earlier.

And then suddenly, out of the silence – because Jenny's fan club was now for the most part engaged in studying their shoes – Bell End yelled, 'Jerzy Pawlowski! Eight ways of moving forward! How many have you got, Kelly? You big girl's blouse! Daisy-chain fairy! Girlie wimp!' he taunted me.

It was as if with that taunt, time stopped just for a millionth of a second, time enough for the talent of Jerzy Pawlowski to well up within me and carry me forward into a flawless advance which was *almost* too late into Jenny's counter-attack. It was in that *almost*, though, that everything happened.

Suspended in that moment, my mind stopped. The world off the piste ceased to exist. I pivoted my body and blade a fraction of a centimetre from Jenny's counter-attack with the elegance of a dancer. Her blade missed me so narrowly, I could hear it *whoosh* past my ear.

In the second it took her to realise that her *flawless* counter-attack had been flawed, I had already snapped my arm into a blinding riposte. Feeling the satisfying *thwack* as my blade made contact on her *lamé,* I heard the hit registering the electronic buzz that proclaimed my victory.

NINE

Even Toxic Psycho Toffs Can Talk Sense, Occasionally

The first thing I wanted to do as the victory light buzzed above my head – apart from taking off my mask – was text Freds. Sister Regina, Sarah and Bell End were a compelling fan club, but it was Freds I wanted to scoop me up into his arms – after a shower anyway.

Over the deafening roar of the crowd because now EVERYONE was cheering *me*, I looked around and saw it might be a while before I was left alone long enough with my mobile to text Freds. I think Bell End was even more thrilled by my victory than I was. Jenny was very sweet too, even when Bell End pushed her away like a stray dog and attempted a non-sexual manly hug with me. With Sister Regina and Sarah hanging off him, though, things didn't go as planned, and we all landed in a tangled heap on the floor.

'Need a hand, darling?' Portia asked, bemused.

'My guardian angel,' I said, reaching my hand out to her.

'Me? I saw the last bit, darling, and believe me, you do *not* need an angel to protect you.' She was laughing as she pulled me out of the tangle of bodies, nun habits and banners and hugged my sweaty head. 'And what was Bell End on?' she asked. 'We could hear him over at the Boys' end. Incredible. I'm sure poor Sister didn't have a clue what she was singing. At least, I hope not.'

I spotted Billy standing behind her, grinning madly. 'Bloody brilliant, Kelly. Where'd you learn to do that?'

'Jerzy Pawlowski,' I explained in a South African accent, but only Portia got the joke.

'Best bloody sabreur that ever lived!' Bell End announced with a slight wobble in his voice. I watched him affectionately as he roughly wiped away a tear trickling down his cheek. 'That's my girl!' he told me gruffly as he stood up and squeezed my shoulder. 'That's my bloody girl! I'll make an Olympian of you, girl. I'll get you gold.'

Sister and Sarah had helped one another up, and Sister was marvelling at what the power of prayer could do. 'Not that you weren't a terrific little swordplayer, Calypso, but heavens, well, simply remarkable! The other nuns will eat their habits when I regale them with the events of today.'

Sarah hugged me as well and told me how proud she was – without reverting to baby-talk – and then she pinched my cheeks really, really hard. It was mortifying, having my mad madre gripping my cheeks while all around people snickered. One moment the champion, the next a figure of fun.

I was rescued by Bell End, who took me aside briefly. 'And don't think it's only me who noticed your talent today, girl,' he whispered. Then he pointed around the hall. 'Spies and scouts are everywhere.'

I looked around the hall where the girls and their fans were gathering their gear and preparing to leave and the boys were still fencing. 'That's why I want to get going quickly, before they can get to you,' he said, tapping his nose.

'But why do they want to get to me? What do they want?'

'You, Kelly. You, damn it. You might be a remarkable sabreur, but you're not the sharpest tool in the box, are you, Kelly?'

'But what do they want me for?' I asked, confused.

'Sponsorship deals, advertising. But don't worry, they're not going to get you. At least not today,' he explained darkly, tapping the side of his nose again. 'We've whet their appetite, though, haven't we, Kelly?'

'Yes, sir,' I agreed, putting his madness down to a long and exhaustive bout of inflicting abuse on poor Jenny and her fans.

'We've whet their appetites good and proper.' Then he threw his head back and laughed like a lunatic. He really had lost his marbles, poor man.

On the journey back, everyone chatted excitedly about the tournament. Bell End was especially proud of his spine-chilling attack on Jenny and her fans. He kept asking questions like, 'And did you see their faces when I yelled, "Spit down the little hamster's throat"!'

'Oh yes, Mr Wellend! Your imaginative *bon mots* really seemed to discourage the other side,' agreed Sister.

'Well, I had a fantastic back-up chorus,' he said, giving Sister and Sarah their due. Portia was unusually chatty as she shared the details of her own victories and defeats. Although I had won the tournament, Portia had distinguished herself sufficiently to give rise to Bell End's hopes that she'd also make it to the Nationals.

Our excitement levels hadn't dropped when we finally got the chance to tell our friends about the day. After we returned from supper slops, Star insisted that we have a tuck fest to celebrate, and Portia and I were happy to repeat our tales of victory once more. Even Portia was animated beyond her usual regal demeanour and acted out some of Sister Regina and my mother's maddest antics. We were high on the whole adventure, and with a pile of sweets on the floor nothing was likely to bring us down any time soon. Even Honey – who sat by the window smoking cigarette after cigarette – couldn't dent my excitement.

'We're definitely coming to the next tournament,' Star insisted firmly.

'Definitely,' agreed the others – even Honey.

Indie laughed. 'Sorry, I keep thinking of your mother and Sister Regina and that banner. We'll have to make our own banner!'

Portia and I looked across at one another in solidarity. The fact of the matter was, Bell End, Sarah and Sister Regina had actually done us proud.

'Yes, let's all go,' Honey added in syrupy tones, stubbing

out her cigarette on the window sill and spraying the room with Febreze. 'It sounds like fun. I want to be there next time to see you rinse the competition. And Bell End sounds hilarious. We could all join him in insulting your competition.'

'I think he's got that side of things under control,' Portia said as she suppressed a smile.

Honey continued. 'It must have felt fantastic, Calypso, winning the tournament like that. I'm seriously impressed. You and Portia deserved to win.'

'Thanks, Honey,' I replied, surprised by the genuine warmth in her congratulations.

'Although, with all this time you're putting into your sabre, it's natural that your other subjects *will* suffer.' She flopped on to her bed, grabbed her *Tatler* and pretended to be absorbed by an article.

Once again I'd been too hasty in thanking her for her warm wishes.

'Not that failing GCSEs matters, darling, well, not to the rest of us,' she added, without looking up from her magazine. 'Between Daddy's plastic and Mummy's contacts, we'll all be fine,' she assured me. Then she looked up at me through the curtain of her implausibly long lashes and added, 'But you don't have a trust fund of your own do you, Calypso?' Her collagen-inflated lower lip wobbled as if she were truly moved by the pathos of my plight. As if she really were about to burst into tears at my lack of plastic and contacts.

As ever, Star came to my rescue. This time with a bag of sugared almonds. 'Almond?' she offered Honey sweetly, holding out a pink-coated nut, knowing full well that Honey was allergic to nuts. Once the 'idiot chavs in the kitchen' had added nuts to a pudding, and she'd had to be rushed to hospital and been kept in for a week on a drip. The school was forced to sack all the 'idiot chavs in the kitchen' for fear of a legal suit. That was back in the days when Honey was still sticking Post-it notes on my back declaring me an American Freak.

Honey shoved away the proffered nut. 'But perhaps money doesn't matter to an American wild child like you, Calypso?' she continued, looking innocently into my eyes. 'You can always make Freddie pay your way, can't you?'

'Pack it in, Honey,' Portia warned.

'Yes, once Calypso wins the essay-writing competition, she'll get a book deal. Unlike you, she doesn't need to rely on Daddy's plastic and Mummy's contacts. She's got something you don't even understand. Talent,' Star said.

As if set off by satanic forces, my text alert sounded.

CONGRATS ON YOUR VICTORY. F

Merde! I hadn't rung Freddie! Billy must have told him about my victory. All I could think of as I read and reread the message – apart from what a horrible girlfriend I was – was the distinct lack of kisses. I should have been the one to tell him. Billy would have told him about Sarah too, and about the madness of the 'Go Boojie! Go!' banner. Fantastic. Just fantastic.

Star and Indie, who were sitting on either side of me, looked at the message. Arabella and Clemmie clambered over to have a look too.

'No kisses,' Arabella noted.

I showed Portia, who grimaced. 'You should have texted him immediately. Billy would have told him as soon as he got back.'

I was already punching in a reply.

CHEERS, WE JUST GOT BACK. I TRIED TO TEXT EARLIER BUT NO SIGNAL, SOZ. XXX C

Before pressing 'Send', I held the message up for a group opinion.

Star shook her head. 'Too lame,' she announced as she snatched the phone from me and changed the message.

ONLY HALF THE VICTORY WITHOUT YOU THERE TO WITNESS. C U IN W TOMOZ? XXXXXX C

'Better,' Indie agreed, holding up the message for every-one else.

'But aren't you going to Windsor with Sarah?' Portia remarked, only she asked too late. Star, being Star, had already pressed 'Send'.

Freddie's reply came back at once.

C U TOMOZ. F XXX

'See!' Star trilled. 'You have to be more assertive with boys, darling. Look at Kevin, he's the perfect boyfriend. Well, just about perfect. I still have some work to do on him musically.'

Kevin was Billy's younger brother and quite possibly the sweetest boy we knew. He was putty in Star's hand and openly worshipped the ground she walked on. Even with Star's wilful charm, I could *never* have that sort of relation-ship with Freddie. These heir-to-the-throne types like to keep a certain amount of power in their relationships. Kevin might enjoy Star's tantrums (well, we all did – she was hilariously outrageous in her treatment of boys) but Freds was not, and never would be, Kev. He was heir to the throne and would never settle for being number two in a relationship.

I took my mobile and stared at Fred's message. Even with three kisses, my fate was sealed – only not in a good way. Sarah was about to collide with the love of my life. A vision of her chasing Freddie through the streets of Windsor with a question-and-answer form and a camera flashed through my mind.

As tired as I was, I knew I was not going to sleep well that night. In addition to the collision course with disaster, Honey's words continued to haunt me. I suppose during all my years of dreaming of making it to the Nationals, I hadn't really considered what that might mean to my grades. To girls like Honey and, well, all the other girls I knew, grades were not an issue. They could pursue their dreams with trust funds.

Honey might be a toxic toff but she still had a solid point. While I focused all my energy on fencing, it was inevitable that my grades would suffer. The GCSE exams were in six months, and my attention was spread very thin indeed, stretched as it was between Sarah and Bob's marital problems, my dream of being a sabreur *par excellence*, and snog-aging my way back into Fred's affections. I hadn't even factored in my GCSEs.

But Honey had. Bob was right when he said even liars tell the truth sometimes. The essay competition and its prize money was starting to seem like an increasingly attractive (if not essential) idea. After all, I had always wanted to be a writer. Maybe the essay competition wasn't such a bad idea. It might even be my big chance at having a proper writing career someday.

TEN

Royal Collision
in Windsor

S arah wore a Chanel suit to Mass the next morning. Not that there weren't other mothers in Chanel suits that morning. In fact, it's a mother's virtual uniform at Saint Augustine's School for Young Ladies. What scared me was that Sarah does not wear Chanel suits, ever. I didn't even know she owned one. The only suits Sarah usually wears are tracksuits. I don't know how she used to dress when she grew up in England, but since living in LA, she had definitely clung to the casual dress code – like latex shorts to an athlete.

Her hair, blond like mine, was normally tied back in a ponytail, just in case she suddenly had an urge to jog somewhere. But now here she was in the chapel as we filed in, pink Chanel suit, matching pink Chanel shoes and bag and hair arranged artfully in a chignon. At six foot tall she looked like a pink stork.

As soon as my Year began to file in, she began to jump about and wave frantically. Presumably she was worried I might miss her loud cries of 'Calypso! Calypso! Darling! Boojems! Over here!'

Throughout Mass, she kept putting her arm around me as if I might escape (the thought did occur to me). She sang her hymns louder than anyone else, cuddled me like I was two and called out 'Ah-men' twice during the sermon. Honey, who was sitting in the row in front, kept turning around and giving her little smiles and winks of encouragement.

I pinched Sarah on the arm over a dozen times to pull her into line. It was as if she had totally forgotten what a toxic witch Honey was. It was only about six months ago that Sarah and Bob flew over from LA to rescue me from one of Honey's poisonous pranks.

As if reading my mind, Honey cast me a look of smug, evil intent, which Sarah totally missed because she was singing reverently with her eyes tightly closed.

After Mass, Sarah swooped down on Sister Constance. 'Oh, Sister!' she cried ecstatically, grasping both Sister's hands and clasping them to her bosom. 'I just want to say how super it is to be back here. It is as if time has stood still. Frozen in that moment of pure joy that defined my years here at Saint Augustine's. It really is just like old times.' She spoke so loudly that Sister Constance could have heard her from a mile away. Everyone stared. Even the Year Sevens. I wanted to shrink up and die of embarrassment.

'Is your mother on medication, darling?' Honey asked with faux concern.

'Shouldn't you be running along, Honey?' Star said,

giving her a pinch and a shove. 'You wouldn't want to be late for your black mass now, would you!'

'Oh, Star,' Honey replied, still managing to ooze sarcasm while rubbing her pinched arm. 'Has your hilarity no end, darling?'

Star gave her a wrist burn, and Star is famous for the brutality of her burns. 'Guess not, *darling*,' she replied mildly, as Honey wrestled back her injured wrist.

'Ouch! Sister! Star just burned me –' Honey wailed, but Sister Constance didn't hear her cry for help because Sarah was moving into her conversational third gear.

'Sarah does seem on madly good form for a woman who's brokenhearted after running off on her husband,' Star whispered in my ear. '*Is* it possible that she is on medication, darling? My mother is, so I'm soooo not judging or anything.'

'I honestly don't know,' I whispered back. 'But she's been reverting since she got here and that's why I don't want to bump into Freddie while I'm with her,' I explained. 'If you see Kevin can you make up a lie about how I couldn't make it into Windsor because I had to, erm –'

'Darling, you shock me. Of course you can meet Freddie, and anyway, you can't ask someone to lie in the house of God!' Star teased as she put her arm around me supportively. 'Besides, Freddie's a big boy, he's going to be king one day, so I'm sure he'll be able to manage Sarah even if she is a bit more bonkers than usual.'

That's Star's philosophy with boys. She considers them charming fools, like circus tumblers placed on this earth for the amusement of girls. I wish I was more like Star, strong and unimpressed by the opposite sex. But I wasn't. Freds made my knees knock, my face redden and my hands shake. I didn't want to risk his feelings for me by exposing him to Sarah in the state she was in.

'Besides, Sarah's a laugh,' Star assured me, giving me another supportive hug. 'I bet he'd love to meet her.'

Sarah had hired a car, a horrible chav car, a true vehicle of shame. Not just because it was a chav-mobile but because, after all her years in LA driving automatics, Sarah had lost the art of using gears. As we crunched and bunny-hopped into Windsor, she cursed all the cars behind us leaning on their horns. She was just like a true American.

'Aw, shut up you Limey arseholes!' she bellowed out the window.

It was the first time I'd seen her criticise the English since she'd arrived. Suddenly things weren't so 'super'. I took a strange comfort in this and relaxed into my seat. Maybe she wasn't on medication, after all.

We decided to have lunch in the pizza place I'd first gone to with Freddie. I knew it was too early for Freddie to eat. In fact it was probably the safest place to hide from him in Windsor. I flashed back to the last time I'd been there with him, and remembered how he had kissed me under an awning as we took shelter from the rain. Today it was crisp and bright.

'What a super day. I love the sunlight of England, don't you?' Sarah asked passionately, looking up as a feeble ray of light broke through the sullen grey sky.

'Erm, well, it's a pretty rare occurrence, but yaah, I guess.'

She clutched my hand and looked into my eyes like a child that's had too many E-numbers. 'Let's both have a large-size, thick-crust pizza with lashings of cheese and pepperoni.'

'What about the carbs!' I cried out in shock. My parents view carbohydrates with the same suspicion other parents view drugs.

'Oh, don't be such a stick-in-the-mud, Boojie. How often do I get to have my baby all to myself, hey?' she asked as she reached out and pinched my cheek.

'Ow!' I rubbed my cheek. 'Look, Sarah, could you *not* call me Boojie?' I insisted a little more brusquely than I meant to.

Sarah looked like she might cry.

I softened my tone. 'At least not in public. It's kind of babyish and, well, you haven't called me Boojie since I was little.' I have never felt soooo horrible. I could see she was about to tear up and, after all, this was a difficult time for her.

'I haven't done a lot of things since you were a little girl, Calypso,' she almost sobbed. 'That's why I'm here. Your father has oppressed me for so long, and now I feel like I have a second chance. Bunny thinks this could be an opportunity to find the *real* me.'

'The *real* you?'

'Yes, the *real* Sarah!'

'I don't understand. If *you're* not the *real* Sarah . . .' I stopped myself before I said, 'you're barking.' 'And who on

earth is Bunny and why would you listen to anything someone with a name like Bunny has told you?' I demanded
crossly.

Sarah looked at me then like *I* was the mad one. 'Oh
darling, try and understand please. I know it's hard on you,
losing your father, but it's hard on me too.'

'Hang on, we haven't lost Bob. You've run off on him!
Because of his Big One.' (I lowered my voice as I said the
words.) 'And what's this about him oppressing you? The
only person in our family who's been oppressed is me, and
you are just as much an oppressor as Bob. Remember the
navel-piercing incident?'

'I was completely supportive of your navel-piercing. It
was Bob who made all the fuss.'

I opened and closed my mouth in shock. Parents are
such liars. And the truth is I think Sarah actually believed
that she *was* all chilled and up for navel-piercing. But I was
there the day she'd attacked the hapless navel-piercer like a
Rottweiler. I remembered, all too clearly, her threat to have
him incarcerated. Sure, Bob had been there finishing off
sentences for her, but she'd been part of the act.

'Have you even called Bob to tell him where you are and
how you feel?' I asked. 'He told me he's almost finished the
script. Maybe if you talked to him –'

'I don't wish to discuss that man. Let's just enjoy one
another, darling. Let's have some real mother and daughter
time.'

Her overuse of the word 'real' was really starting to
bother me, almost as much as her use of my baby name.

'Well, he's still my father even if he is a slow writer.' I sulked. 'And what do you mean by *real*, Sarah? What other sort of time would we have?' I asked her even though it was all feeling a bit *surreal* to me.

'Well, you know, real as in, *real*.' She struggled a bit more to explain what 'real' actually meant, and then she went quiet and looked dazed, almost dopey, just like a woman on medication.

I had to ask. 'Look, Sarah, Mummy, can I ask you something? Something, well, personal?'

Sarah looked dementedly excited by this prospect. 'Oh, Calypso, ask me anything!' She gestured wildly, almost knocking a passing waiter off his feet. 'I don't want any secrets between us. I want us to have a really, really close mother-daughter bond. I don't want you to feel that you need to speak to a counsellor when I'm here for you. Mummy's here for you now!' She held out her arms expansively. 'Ask me anything.'

The whole restaurant had gone silent and was waiting for me to speak. I bottled out and began fiddling with my napkin. 'It doesn't matter.'

'Have you got your period, darling?' she yelled – well, at least it seemed as if she yelled it, and people *were* looking.

'No!' I replied, horrified.

She patted my hand. 'Well, one day we'll have a special little mother-daughter talk about your pink cycle and how it will change your life forever and turn you into a *real* woman.'

'No, we won't. And anyway, I've been having my period for a year!'

Sarah grabbed my hands and squeezed them. 'Oh, Calypso, how wonderful. You're a real *woman* now!' I thought she was about to break into song but instead she set her mouth in a bitter teenage grimace Honey would have been proud of.

'See, this is what Bob has done to us, don't you see?'

I shook my head, briefly wondering if it was even worth contradicting her. OK, Bob might be a bit wrapped up in his script, but that didn't make him the root of all evil. Despite a sane little voice inside my head that said to let it go, I blurted, 'I don't think you can blame Bob for *that*, Sarah. Besides, I got my first period at school, so what was I supposed to do, send you an e-mail? "Dear Sarah and Bob, I am having my period today"?'

'Can't you see, you should have been able to share something as momentous as that with your own mother? But no, Bob always *had* to be the centre of attention. Bob and his Big . . .' she paused, about to say 'One', but after a short hesitation she said, 'Opus. Your father was like a vacuum of need, and I was always too focused on him when I should have been more focused on you, Calypso. That's what my therapist taught me.'

'Therapist? You're seeing a therapist?' I don't know why I said this when Sarah was giving every indication that she was going gah-gah and in need of professional help. I guess it was a shock, Sarah being so totally boring, grown-up and happy with Bob. Also, it's never easy to find out your own mother is in therapy. Your parents are meant to be rocks of solid purpose in a sea of turmoil.

'Of course I am. Everyone in LA is in therapy,' she declared.

'But you're not gah-gah!' I lied.

'Oh, don't be so English, darling. It was Bunny who suggested I leave Bob and come here to spend more time with you. I still talk to her every day on the phone. She's awfully good, Calypso. She's made me realise how I have always put Bob first and how I have allowed his needs to oppress me all these years.'

'Who is this Bunny woman and how would she know whether or not Bob's oppressed you, Sarah? This is mad. Bob couldn't oppress a fly. He's got his faults, I'll grant you, what with his appalling dress sense and those horrible noises he makes when he eats, but that can't be classed as oppression, even by Hollywood standards.'

'Bunny is my therapist. She warned me that you might become hostile at the news of losing your father so suddenly.'

'I haven't *lost* him. I e-mailed him the other day. And he e-mailed me straight back. He's still my father, even if he is annoying.'

She glared at me and I glared right back, and then I realised the waiter was standing there, and I went bright red.

Sarah took charge, slipping seamlessly from gah-gah loon to her mother superior bossy boots. 'We'll have two large thick-crust pizzas, thank you, double the cheese, double the pepperoni –'

'But I don't want pepperoni,' I interjected.

Sarah ignored me, waving my words away as if I were the mad one. 'Double everything in fact, and triple the carbs!' she insisted, glaring at me in a very oppressive way.

The waiter looked clearly unnerved and turned to me for support. I smiled reassuringly at the poor guy. He was only about nineteen and quite fit, I noticed. 'Two large. One Hawaiian, and one pepperoni and two Diet Cokes,' I told him sweetly. 'And make those *thin* crusts,' I added firmly as I gave Sarah a warning stare.

She didn't say another word until the pizzas arrived, and then she thanked the waiter effusively. We ate our meal in cold silence. I expect she had found this particular mother-daughter bonding session a bit of a let-down. I wondered how she'd describe it to her therapist, Bunny. But then after a while I began to feel bad because, whatever was going on with her and Bob, she was definitely going through a difficult time (although I was starting to think this Bunny might be more responsible than Bob for this whole drama). So as we were leaving the restaurant, I took my mad madre's hand in mine and thanked her for lunch. 'Would you like to have a look around the shops, Sarah?' I suggested brightly, hoping to coax her out of her mood.

She didn't need much encouragement. She wrapped her arm around my waist and gave me a squeeze. 'Sorry if I'm being a bit full on,' she explained. 'It's just that I'm still finding my feet as a single mom.'

I spoke to her gently. 'But Sarah, you're not really a single mom, are you?' I asked. Or was she a single mom, I wondered briefly, remembering the essay competition. 'Bob loves you. I know he can be annoying but he does love us both and he does want you to go home. You two belong together. Who's going to finish off his sentences for him?' There, I'd said it. Bugger Bunny and her nutty therapy.

But Sarah was not so easily persuaded. 'I belong here,' she said, adding 'with you. And you'll adore the house in Clapham, Boojie. It's right on the Common. I can't wait for you and your friends to have your sleepover party on the exeat weekend. I'll pick all of you up and we can go back on the train together. Won't that be super?'

Super. Public transport was not the standard form of conveyance for Saint Augustine girls, but I was certain my friends would be more than happy for the adventure. Apart from Honey, obviously. 'Yaah, that sounds great,' I agreed cheerfully.

'Super. We'll have a real girls' night in!'

'As opposed to one of those faux girls' nights in?' I teased, but my poor madre just looked at me as if I were speaking in tongues again, and then her eyes glazed over the way mad people's do.

'Sarah, you weren't serious about Bob not being part of your emotional therapy thingamee were you?' I asked gently as the sun slipped behind a cloud for what I expected would be a very long visit.

'I don't want to talk about anything serious,' she said gaily. 'I just want to have fun with my Boojie.'

'Boojie?' A voice came from behind. It was Kevin, Star's boyfriend and Freddie's best mate.

'Hel-lo there!' my mother sang – yes *sang*.

'Erm, hello. Kevin Pyke, I'm a friend of Calypso's.' He

extended his hand and gave me a look that said, 'I'm afraid. I want to run away.'

'My name's Sarah, Kevin. I'm Calypso's mummy.' With that, Sarah grabbed Kevin's hand, but not to shake it. Instead, she pulled him along with us down the cobbled lane, swinging his arm in one hand and mine in the other. 'Now, Kevin, I want to hear *all* about you. You and I are going to be super friends, I can just feel it.'

'Yes, Mrs Kelly,' Kevin agreed, but I could tell he was afraid. He kept trying to look me in the eye as a few drops of rain began to fall, but I couldn't face him.

'Isn't this simply super, kids? Don't you just love an English shower!'

Kevin laughed. 'Actually, I think it's about to piss down, Mrs Kelly.'

'Sarah. You must call me Sarah. I don't want you to think of me as some old woman with no idea about current trends, Kevin. I'm a writer on one of your teen shows, *Gladesdale*. So, Kevin, tell me ALL about yourself. I want to know everything. I want to know what makes you tick. I want to know the *real* Kevin.'

'Right. Well there's not much to tell,' he told the mad madre. 'And see the thing is, love to chat and all, but have to run. Meeting the girlfriend, you see.'

Trust Star to be referred to with an article – I wondered if Freds referred to me as *the* girlfriend? I suspected not. I wondered if he even said 'my girlfriend', but I doubted that as well.

'Ooooh, who's the lucky girl, Kevin?' Sarah pried embarrassingly.

'Sarah!' I scolded. 'Don't be such a busybody.'

'Star. She's, erm, a friend of Calypso's. Actually, Calypso will fill you in. I have to leg it or I'll be –'

'Oh, lovely. I know Star well. She came to stay with us in LA when we were still a family . . .' She allowed her voice to trail off as if she couldn't go on, which was sooo not true. She was dying for Kevin to say something sympathetic so she could pour her heart out.

Poor Kevin looked like a fox caught in a trap. 'OK. Well, sounds cool but Star will murder me if I'm late.' He pointed at me as he backed off. 'And Freddie is looking for you too, Calypso. Nice to meet you, Mrs Kelly, I mean Sarah,' he called out as he legged it down the lane.

With that, he was gone and so was my hope of finding a way of pretending to Freds that I hadn't actually made it into Windsor that day.

I was definitely going to have some material for my essay now. My life was looking increasingly tragic by the minute. And then it got really bad. 'Calypso!' Freddie called from the other end of the lane. He looked gorgeous; his dark hair that did funny sticky-out things without gel, still upright despite the increasing rain. I couldn't see his dazzling cornflower blue eyes yet, but I was drawn to him just like the moon is drawn to the earth, or is it the sun, or the other way around? The point it is, I longed to run towards him.

'Is that . . . is that . . . is that?' Sarah repeated, over and over again in a swoon.

My distressingly fit boyfriend began moving towards us.

With each step he took, my mind threw up a thousand reasons why I should resist the overwhelming desperation within me to run for the hills.

My dread of being embarrassed by Sarah won. It took me a split second to grab my mad madre's hand. 'Quick,' I hissed. 'We have to leg it. It's a game we play!' I explained.

'Oh, super,' Sarah squealed as we ran like a pair of bag snatchers down Bond Street. She was laughing and shrieking, probably exhilarated by how teenage and puerile it all was. Or perhaps this event would feature on an episode of *Gladesdale*. Or maybe it was just her medication. Either way, we arrived at her car in a state of soggy, giggly dishevelment.

My life was ruined. I had just run from my boyfriend and, however fit and wonderful Freds was, unlike Sarah, he was not going to see the fun in what I'd just done.

But I didn't have a chance to dwell on how gutted I was inside. I had to distract Sarah so she wouldn't want me to explain why I'd just dragged her away from Freds. It's times like this that blurting actually comes in quite handy. 'There's a competition,' I blagged. I know it was wicked to take advantage of my mother's madness, but I couldn't exactly tell her the truth, could I?

As it was, I didn't need to blag. Sarah was babbling away excitedly about how hilarious and outrageous we were, running off like that on Prince Frederick, as she insisted on calling him. 'Bob would die!' she said and tooted the horn with happiness.

'Definitely,' I lied. 'Now about this essay,' I continued.

'Wasn't it wonderful – the look on his face? I can't wait

to tell Bunny. She's always urging me to be more playful.'

No doubt she would soon start wondering about when she *would* meet Freds, so I was determined to distract her now with talk of the essay competition.

'Yes, so there's this essay-writing competition,' I insisted. 'An autobiographical sort of thing. You know, drawing on one's own life experience, that sort of thing.'

'Oh, Bunny is big on that. She has made me keep a Journal of Pain since I first started seeing her. I write down all the agonies I endure each day. That was how Bunny made me see the pattern of neglect I was suffering at the hands of your father. I'm soooo glad that you are finally able to see the value of committing your pain to paper, darling.'

'Yes,' I agreed uncertainly. 'It's not my usual field, but I think I'm going to have a shot at it. There's really big prize money if you win, and they're publishing the best five in the *Telegraph*, so there will be a lot of recognition.'

'Oh darling, a prize? Imagine if you win? Oh, this is exciting,' she exclaimed, finally tuning in.

'Yaah, well, I don't think my life's been nearly traumatic enough for me to win, but –'

'Boojems! Don't put yourself down. You're life has been full of pain. Shoved off to boarding school, tortured by that dreadful Honey girl, oppressed by an overbearing father and coming from a broken home –'

I cut her off before the violin chorus started up. 'Mmmm, but you see because it is about one's own life experience, it's bound to get, well, quite personal, you know what I mean.' I looked at Sarah for signs of how she might feel about this. Her gaze was fixed on the road. It was raining heavily now, and the wipers were making it difficult to see what was in front of us. Also, she was still having gear stick problems. But I persisted. 'I thought I might write about us, you know, as in my family sort of thing. Like Gerald Durrell – you remember that book, *My Family and Other Animals*. Bob gave it to me when I was six.'

'Yes, darling, you're a very talented writer. You know I support all your creative endeavours.'

'So you don't mind?'

'Why would I mind?'

'No, no, there's no reason you would, but you know it might mean mentioning you and Bob? You are my family, if you see what I am saying?'

'I still don't understand why you think I might mind. The truth will come out. We can't hide our pain under a bushel our entire lives, darling. That's what Bunny says. So you must write this essay. If Bob has a problem, he'll have to claim it as his own. I'm proud of you, Boojie,' she said. And I could tell she meant it. 'So, when do I get to meet this Frederick? We can't keep teasing him like this forever, Boojie.'

'No,' I agreed, my fingers firmly crossed behind my back. 'We can't.'

ELEVEN

The Risk of Taking Your Soft Toys Too Seriously

'You what?' demanded Star, for the thousandth time later that evening after Sarah had dropped me off at school.

'I told you what,' I replied through gritted teeth. 'Look, I'm not proud of it.'

'I think it's hilarious,' Indie said, laughing. She was funny when she laughed, mostly because of the way she put her hand over her mouth as if laughing at something truly shocking, which I suppose legging it from HRH was in a way.

'Sarah enjoyed it,' I added, as if giving my poor mad madre a good time made up for the mess I'd made of my relationship with Freds.

'Only she had no idea that the reason you were running away from the poor guy was because you're so embarrassed by *her*,' Star pointed out bluntly.

My face went bright red. 'That is soooo not true! I'm not embarrassed of Sarah. I love her.'

'Huh. So when you said you were too embarrassed to let

Freddie and Sarah meet in Windsor, you were what? Deranged?' Star does a very good line in logic, which can be really annoying.

'If I was so embarrassed, I would have –'

'Legged it through Windsor? I'm really, really disappointed in you,' Star told me crossly, shaking her head so that her lovely red hair came out of its black leather star-studded hair strap. Every day she looked more and more the quintessential rock chick, which only added further kudos to her fearsome certainty about life and reminded me just how fearsomely uncertain I was about my own.

Indie had stopped laughing now too, which meant Star was even scaring her.

'You're *so* wrapped up in yourself, Calypso, you just don't even see how your actions impact on others! Poor Sarah, and I even feel sorry for his royal stuck-upness. He must have felt a right idiot, standing there in the rain while his girlfriend and her mother legged it down the lane, shrieking with laughter!' Star continued to scold.

'I tried to call Freddie to explain,' I told her, as if that should be an end to it. Not that I knew what I was going to say to him, but the word 'sorry' would definitely have featured. Each time I had dialled he had rejected my call, though. I could picture him, white with fury, pressing the 'Reject Call' button every time the name 'Calypso' came up on his mobile's screen. Maybe he'd even changed my name on his speed dial. I do that when I'm cross with people. Honey came up on my phone as EVIL ONE – not that she ever called me. Still, it gave me a cheap thrill.

I'd even tried texting Freddie.

PLSE STOP REJECTING MY CALLS. I'M REALLY, REALLY SORRY ABOUT THIS AFTERNOON. PLSE LET ME EXPLAIN XXXXXXX C

But he remained unreachable.

Supper was fish nuggets, which I normally fall on like a famine victim, but I couldn't eat a morsel that night. Indie tried to get her security guys to hide the nuggets in their pockets, but they got caught by Sandra, the dinner lady, and I was put on report for not eating my food.

Indie was really sympathetic, as was everyone apart from Star. I hate it when Star is angry with me, because firstly she's always right, and secondly the cold frost she exuded towards me that evening made me shiver.

After supper, Georgina, Clemmie, Arabella, Indie and Star hung out in my room. Everyone apart from Star was trying to come up with a way for me to win Freddie back. Honey was unusually quiet on the subject, and Honey being quiet on a topic that had everyone else gossiping was dangerous.

Eventually, Georgina joined Honey at the window sill to smoke and I tried to listen in to their low murmurings, but I caught only the occasional word like 'erm' and 'yaah' and 'darling'.

Arabella suggested a proper snail mail love letter on lovely embossed paper. 'It's got my family crest on it, but we can cross that out,' she added.

'Yes, what a brilliant idea. You could even be really Victorian and lacy and spray it with your scent, Calypso. I'm sure Freddie would swoon with love, unable to resist a letter explaining why his girlfriend is so embarrassed by the prospect of him and her mother meeting that she runs away at the very sight of him,' Star scoffed.

I felt really annoyed with her for being so bloody right.

Portia was reading a magazine on her bed. She'd given me a look of sympathy, but it wasn't her way to get overly involved in other people's petty problems.

'What about sending him a gorilla-gram? Or his favourite pizza, with your name spelled out in sausage?' Clemmie suggested.

Even Star giggled at this.

I didn't giggle, though. I was truly ashamed of myself, and if my name spelled out in sausage would make things right with Freddie I was all up for trying it.

Georgina pulled her head in from the window. 'Why don't you go and see him face-to-face? You know, storm the ramparts of Eades?'

No one said anything at first. Eades was only a couple of miles away, but it meant climbing down the scaffolding, traversing Puller's Wood, where attack dogs roamed looking for girls to eat, and slithering through the razor-wire fence that shielded our school from the outside world.

'But the attack dogs – you know I'm terrified of attack dogs,' I argued, even though I longed more than anything to confront Freddie face-to-face.

Honey pulled her head in from outside the window and picked up the Febreze. I imagined she was going to spray away the smell of smoke. I don't know how I survive being this naïve, I really don't.

'Which is why,' Honey said, holding the Febreze up and pointing it directly at me, 'you take my mace to defend yourself.' With that she squirted the Febreze right in my eyes, which made them sting and water like crazy.

'Honey!' Georgina scolded, snatching the spray from her friend.

'What? I was just showing her what she can do if the dogs pitch up and start tearing her apart,' Honey explained in a voice of child-like innocence as I rinsed my eyes out with water from the sink.

'Well, I think it's a perfect idea. Tobias suggested it earlier,' Georgina told us, holding her bear up. His wise face stared back at us solemnly. 'He's given it a lot of thought.'

I looked at Star, expecting her to roll her eyes, but instead she said, 'Right, so here's the plan. After lights out, we'll all convene here and help you escape. I'll text Kevin to get directions to Freddie's room and find out the best access routes.'

'Billy mentioned there's wisteria running along the wall where Freddie's housed,' Portia added.

I looked at everyone's supportive faces.

'You can borrow my black trackie bums and black hoodie,' Clemmie offered.

All their faces were expectant. Honey was rustling about in the en suite. When she appeared, she pressed a small can of mace into my hand.

'Thank you,' I muttered, looking at the can. It had a cartoon picture of a girl spraying a man in the face.

'No trouble; Mummy bought it for me in Germany, you

know, in case Miss Bibsmore gets too much for me. But don't accidentally squirt yourself in the dark, darling. It isn't Febreze, remember.' She laughed her crazed laugh at the memory.

'Right,' I agreed, still staring at the can because actually I am just the sort of girl who would squirt herself in the face with mace.

'Promise you'll only use it if the dog is *really* going to endanger your life?' Clemmie insisted sternly. She can't bear to think of any creature being hurt. She even hates it when we eat Jelly Babies, because she says they remind her of her little brother Sebastian.

'Of course I won't.' I sooo would, though, if the jaws of a dog were bearing down on me.

Star came over and gave me a hug. 'I'm really proud of you,' she said.

'You're doing the right thing,' Portia agreed.

'We'd better leg it back to our own rooms now, though,' Star said. 'We'll come back after Miss Bibsmore's done her rounds to help you get ready, OK?'

I nodded. I was mute with the enormity of the mission I was about to embark upon. A mission conceived by a soft toy. A mission which, if anything went wrong, could very easily end in my expulsion. But Freds was worth it. I hoped.

TWELVE

Scaling the Battlements of Eades

At eleven that night, Star and Portia climbed down the scaffolding with me, while Honey, Indie and Georgina watched from above, shining their torches on us.

Star and Portia said they'd come with me as far as the razor wire in case there was a serious emergency. Portia had drawn a map, which I tucked safely in my Snoopy bra – the closest thing I had to a sports bra. It was still raining, which Star pointed out was all the more incentive to run faster.

Things went well on the wet sprint through the school grounds, but no sooner were we in the woods than four attack dogs came bounding out at us like the hounds of hell. Star grabbed one by the collar and Portia grabbed another, but with my fear of dogs being what it is, all I could do was grab the trunk of a tree and start climbing. The two untethered dogs growled and snarled up at me.

'Climb down, you're setting them off,' Star called up to me.

'I'm setting *them* off?' I called down. 'They're the ones barking and baying for my blood.'

'Only because they sense your fear.'

'Well, I'm bloody afraid.'

'Here boy!' Star called to the dogs and, when they came to her, she fed them some sweets.

'Now, Calypso, now!' Portia urged. 'Sugared almonds won't hold them back forever.'

So I jumped down and legged it through the woods. My torch gave only enough light to keep me from running into trees, but hearing the footfalls of Portia and Star as they came up behind me made me feel braver. I was running so fast the effects of missing supper resulted in a stitch by the time we reached the razor wire, which looked as if it would tear us to ribbons.

'OK, this is where we have to veer left,' Portia said, panting. Star continued to sprint purposefully ahead, running parallel to the wire.

'Or go back?' I suggested, only half joking as I held my side.

'According to Billy there's a green ribbon on the wire and after that a bush which conceals where the wire has a gap in it. That's where you'll slip through,' she added, ignoring my lame attempt at humour.

'Here it is,' called Star. When we caught up to her voice, it was coming from inside the bush. She looked so unlike a rock chick as her face peered out from the bush that I almost lost my fear.

'You'll be fine now. Kev and Billy are both expecting you.

Billy's going to text you if there's a problem,' Portia reminded me.

'So make sure your mobile's on vibrate. Kev will keep a lookout over the house. Remember it's the second house, second row on the right, after Chapel Row,' Star whispered.

'That's right, just keep your eye out for Poets Well,' Portia reminded me.

'Right, Poets Well. Eyes out,' I repeated.

'Because if you see that, you've gone too far,' she said.

I was already thinking I had gone too far.

'Good luck, and once you've sorted things out with Freddie, text us and we'll be here to meet you, OK?'

I was drenched to the skin and hungry and my stitch was killing me as my friends disappeared through the woods. Worst of all I was alone in the dark.

After I struggled through the prickly bush, I looked out at the foreboding glow of spires and ancient gabled roofs of Eades all lit up by security lighting. A sense of hopelessness came over me, but there was no turning back now – well, not without a major confrontation with Star. So I moved through the pain the way I'd been taught to in fencing and sprinted towards the boarding houses, clutching Honey's mace in one hand and my mobile in the other.

I repeated Star's directions in my head, second house, second row, and right after the chapel. Whoops, was that turn right *at* the chapel, though, or right *after* the chapel? I decided the best course of action was to check my map, but in the heavy rain that was easier said than done.

I took shelter against a wall when I saw a security guard

lighting up a cigarette farther down at one of the houses. That was when I noticed that the wall I was leaning against had wisteria growing over it. Portia had mentioned wisteria, so this must be it. I looked up, wondering if Freddie was up there. There were lights on and noises of boys talking or listening to televisions and music. At least up there I'd be out of the rain, which was really pissing down now, and surely some nice Eades boy would take me to my prince?

I grabbed hold of a wisteria branch and tugged hard to check it could support my weight before slipping my foot into one of the branches and hoisting myself up. It was actually quite easy, and I was almost feeling a bit smug and action heroine-ish there for a moment as I scaled the wall of Eades. And then I reached the first floor window, looked down and realised I was above Poets Well. 'Bugger,' I swore to myself. 'Calypso Kelly, you have gone too far.'

A window opened just above my head and a boy's face, a cigarette clenched between his lips, looked down on me.

'Hello there. What was that you were saying?'

'Oh, hi,' I said, smiling my most winning smile. 'I'm sort of looking for someone.'

'Not me, is it?' the face asked.

'No, someone else.'

'Jolly good, well, good luck. I hope you manage to track him down,' the boy said, before pulling his head back in and slamming the window shut.

The wisteria wasn't feeling quite as stable as it had earlier. I think in my rain-drenched clothing I was probably twice as heavy as I normally was. I looked down on Poets Well and tried to find the bottle to climb back down and work out another way to Freddie's house. I sneezed really, really loudly. Not one of those public, polite sneezes either – you know the ones where people add 'God bless you' afterwards. No, this was a roaring loud sneeze that was probably heard back at Saint Augustine's. Normally I would only allow a sneeze like that to escape when I was certain I was all alone in a completely embarrassment-proof environment.

I heard the window opening above me again. 'God bless you.' The face from earlier reappeared. 'You sure you're not cold out there?'

I looked up, no longer capable of smiling, winningly or otherwise. 'Bloody freezing,' I admitted.

'Are you sure I won't do? As an interim measure, perhaps? At least it's warm in here, if you don't mind a bit of a mess.'

I was so relieved I almost let go my grip on the wisteria. 'Thank you,' I gushed as his hand reached down and my stranger pulled me up and helped me climb into his room.

THIRTEEN

You've Got to Know When to Neck It and When to Leg It

'**M**y name's Malcolm, by the way. Feel free to use the bathroom to dry yourself off.' He was wearing boxer shorts with a rugby shirt over the top. With his thatch of red hair and green eyes, he reminded me of Star. He was definitely the best thing to happen to me in the last half hour, I decided.

'Thanks. I'm Calypso,' I said as my eyes travelled around the vast room. I knew that Eades boys all got their own rooms, but I had never been in one before. It was the size of most people's living rooms. He had a plasma screen television, DVD, laptop and of course the mess he had warned me of. Actually most of the mess seemed to consist of thousands of DVDs strewn all over the floor – and I mean *all* over the floor. Every square inch was covered in DVDs, including the square inches I was currently dripping on.

'Actually, I'll grab you a towel. I think we'd better contain you,' Malcolm said, treading his way carefully to the bathroom so as to avoid stepping on the DVDs. From the bathroom he chucked me a big black fluffy towel. I began to dab at my sodden clothing and hair in a hopeless attempt to dry myself off.

'Tell you what, Calypso,' Malcolm said. 'Chuck the towel down over the DVDs and once you get to the bathroom you can climb out of those wet clothes and put on my robe. It's virtually clean. If you like, you can spread your clothes over my radiators while we find your mystery man.'

'Thank you, that's really kind,' I said as I made my way towards the bathroom. I was feeling slightly uncomfortable about taking my clothes off in a boy's bathroom and changing into his robe, even if it was virtually clean. I mean, I didn't even know Malcolm. What if he were some sort of crazed rapist, or worse? As I opened the bathroom door I turned round, but he was crouched on the floor with his back to me, totally absorbed in some sort of laborious DVD filing process. It was as if he'd forgotten all about my existence in his room.

The bathroom wasn't as luxurious as our bathroom back at Saint Augustine's. The tiling was a bit chipped and the mirror was so old it was all speckled. But it was such a relief to pull off my wet clothes that I decided I was mad to be so paranoid. Malcolm's robe was a green-and-maroon-striped Ralph Lauren affair and, best of all, it was deliciously clean, fluffy and two sizes too big for me.

I gathered up my sodden clothes and walked back into the room as if everything were perfectly natural and normal.

'Drink?' Malcolm offered without looking up as I began to lay my clothes on his piping hot radiators.

'Yaah, a drink would be super,' I drawled, cringing at my ridiculous blurt. Super? Was I turning into my mother?

'Help yourself. The fridge is over there,' Malcolm told me as he gestured to the other side of the room. 'If everything doesn't fit on that radiator, there's another along the bed.

'Thanks,' I replied, cringing with embarrassment as I spread my wet Snoopy bra and knickers over the radiator behind his bed. I looked over at Malcolm but, as he wasn't showing anything more than a courteous disinterest in me, I figured it would be OK. I mean, they'd probably be dry in ten minutes and then I could get dressed and find Freds.

I placed my mobile and mace on the fridge.

'Sorry, excuse the poor selection. I'm not much of a drinker, I'm afraid,' Malcolm explained without looking up from his chore.

I opened the glass fridge door and suddenly it was like being back in Honey's limo again. It was full of miniature bottles of Veuve Clicquot. 'I could probably get one of the other guys to dig you up some vodka if you'd prefer?' he suggested, no doubt imagining that I was disappointed by his unvaried selection.

I didn't want to sound babyish and admit I actually thought he was offering me a Horlicks or something nice and sweet like that, so I said it was fine and took a bottle out.

'Should I, erm, open one for you?' I asked, uncertain of the etiquette rules of Eades boys and their fridges.

'Cheers,' he said, smiling at me as he ran his fingers through his hair in what looked like frustration. 'I shouldn't, but this is going to be a long night.'

I uncorked the two small bottles pretty skilfully, proving that even time spent in the company of someone as poisonous as Honey has its uses.

Malcolm placed his champagne beside him on the floor. He seemed too absorbed in his DVDs to care where I sat, so I perched on the edge of his bed. I still felt madly awkward, so I decided to spread out and look a bit more chilled as I took a gulp of the champagne. Instantly all the bubbles charged up my nose and I started choking and coughing.

'Unlike beer, it's better not to neck your champagne like that,' Malcolm suggested, suppressing a laugh. 'It's easier if you use the straw that's glued to the side,' he explained, pointing out the straw.

'Oh yaah, no, of course I know that. It's just, well, I prefer to knock it back, really,' I blurted in a blatantly ridiculous attempt at sounding sophisticated. And once I started I couldn't stop. 'Hic, hic, hic,' was my next sophisticated blurt. My plan to look all chilled and worldly was sinking fast.

'So who is it exactly that you are looking for?' Malcolm asked in a tone that suggested he was keen to be rid of the strange, wet girl hiccuping in his room.

'*Hic, hic, hic,*' I replied.

'Do you need something for your hiccups? A paper bag? A fright perhaps?' he asked, looking around his room for a solution.

He didn't have to look far, though. Before I could *hic* another word out, Portia's older brother, Tarquin, stormed into the room.

'Have you found that bloody DVD yet, McHamish?' Tarquin demanded crossly before he noticed me, stretched out across Malcolm's bed in a robe. He only gave me a cursory glance, but I clutched the robe to my neck as I imagined what he might be thinking.

'Still looking, man – the search goes on. I will be triumphant, though! I will be triumphant,' Malcolm declared, punching the air with his mini-bottle of Veuve.

By this point Tarquin had not only spotted me *hic, hic, hic*ing away on Malcolm's bed, but he'd also taken in my matching Snoopy bra and knickers (thank goodness I'd taken the precaution of wearing matching underwear, otherwise it could have been *really* embarrassing) flung over the radiator.

'Briggs, meet Calypso, she who would lure men from their whatsits.'

'Goals. Listen, I know you,' Tarquin said, pointing to me as if he wished he didn't. 'You're that friend of Portia's. Freddie's girlfriend.'

'*Hic*, yes, *hic*, yes. Nice to, *hic*, see, *hic*, you again, *hic*,' I replied giving him a little wave.

'She's been necking her champagne,' Malcolm explained, gesturing to me with his champagne. 'That's how she prefers to drink it apparently. I told her to use a straw, but girls, what can you do?' He shrugged.

I pulled Malcolm's robe even more tightly around me, suddenly acutely aware of how naked I was underneath.

The next minute, Billy burst in on my humiliation. 'Right McHamish, where's the bloody –' He stopped short as he spotted me. He looked confused. 'Calypso? What's going on?'

'*Hic*, well, you, *hic*, I was . . .'

'Ah Pyke, my good man. Yes, your DVD is on the fridge.'

But Billy didn't seem to be interested in the whereabouts of his DVD. 'What are you doing *here*? In Malcolm's room?' he asked me irritably.

'Ah, the fair Calypso. Everyone seems to know this young wench. Found her hanging off my window sill, wet as a drowning rat. Said she could dry herself off before she continued her search for, what was his name again?'

'Freds!' I squeaked – yes, squeaked, like one of those soft toys babies have. Because I wasn't answering Malcolm's question at all. Freds had just walked in and he did not look pleased to see me. Not a bit. If looks could burn, my matching Snoopy bra and knickers would have burst into flames, because his eyes were boring into them. I jumped up off the bed, desperate to explain the situation but all that came out was '*Hic*'.

Malcolm must have been the only one unaware of the dynamics of the drama being played out in his room. 'Now Freds, I've got your DVD, I think I put it –' Malcolm began, but Freds turned around and walked straight back out again, muttering something about how he couldn't believe this.

Well bugger that, the fighter in me said! I hadn't fought

off attack dogs, wriggled through razor-wire fences, run through the rain and climbed wisteria bushes for nothing. No, I, Calypso Kelly, sabre champion of the Sheffield Open, was not giving up. I stuffed the mace and phone in one of the pockets of the robe, grabbed my Snoopy set and clothes and legged it after him.

That was when I ran into the Eades house matron, spilling my champagne all over her and me and, well, that was when things got really nasty.

Malcolm, Billy and Tarquin, who had also given chase, slammed into the matron and me.

'Aaah, good. I see you've met our matron, Kate. Kate, this is Calypso, she who distracts men from their –'

Kate just stared at him. 'Thank you, Mr McHamish, you can go back to your room.'

Billy and Tarquin followed him and that was that. I was alone with Kate, who in her twinset and pearls looked terrifyingly formidable.

FOURTEEN

Matron's Remedy for Hiccups

'There's a perfectly reasonable explanation for this,' I told Kate, trying to sound as authoritative as Honey and as aloof as Portia. But in addition to my lack of attire, I was also buckling under the additional hurt of Freds storming off. Talk about taking the wind out of a girl's sails.

The matron gripped me by the robe and, robes being what they are, I didn't even try to argue or struggle because, well, having a near-naked girl on her hands is at least a little better than an actual naked girl. Also, I still had the hiccups.

Malcolm's head popped out of his door. 'Any chance you can bring the robe back on your next visit, Calypso?' he asked.

Kate turned around to face him, and a horrible sense of doom came over me − not that I wasn't already feeling doom-ish enough about the evening's events, but I didn't want to land Malcolm in any sort of trouble when he'd been so hospitable.

'Where does this girl come from, Mr McHamish?' Kate enquired nicely, in the sort of voice one might ask the time.

'Good question, Kate. I have no idea of her origins. I did think I detected a slight transatlantic accent when I first came across her. She was hanging, wet as a stray cat, on the wisteria outside my window, looking for some chap. I invited her in to dry off before she continued her search.'

By the time he had finished his explanation, Billy, Tarquin and a few other boys had opened their doors to watch the scene.

'I see,' said Kate. 'Well, do any of you chaps know where she's from?' she put it to the ever-increasing number of boys coming out to have a look at me.

I felt myself shrinking inside the robe. 'My name's, *hic*, Calypso,' I told her quietly. '*Hic*, Calypso Kelly.'

'She's from Saint Augustine's,' Billy offered.

'A friend of my sister's,' Tarquin added darkly.

'Well, I'd better ring Sister Constance and inform her that I'm driving you back to school, Miss Kelly. It's a good thing our Head is in bed along with all the rest of the beaks.' Then she turned to the boys. 'Good night, gentlemen. And Mr McHamish, please don't smoke in the corridor; you know it's against fire regulations.'

'Right, yes, blast the bloody regulations. Such a lot of rot.' He smiled at Kate, took a drag of his cigarette and stubbed it out on the floor and then took a sip of his champagne.

I was astonished that Kate didn't scold him, but clearly Eades boys had more power when it came to matrons than we did.

The boys all said good night to Kate as if she were an employee. Billy thanked her for looking after me, which made me feel like a stray dog. Then they all shut their doors, and I was alone with Kate.

As I looked at her and she looked at me, I began to fear repercussions. My brave adventure had come to a soggy and miserable failure of an end. Far from convincing Freds of my undying affection, I had totally alienated him.

Kate didn't say anything to me. She led me downstairs to her office, where she called Sister Constance. 'I have one of your girls here,' she explained. I couldn't hear what Sister said to Kate, but I imagined her attitude to the situation wouldn't be as casual as Kate's. 'No, no, that's fine, Sister. I'll drive her back,' Kate continued. 'Only three minutes away.'

Three minutes of terror away! Kate drove like a maniac. Her driving made Sister Regina's seem safe in comparison, and Sister Regina is too short to see over the wheel. I could see over the wheel, though, as we sped around hairpin bend after hairpin bend.

One good thing about her reckless driving was that it made speaking impossible and proved to be just the fright I needed to rid myself of the wretched hiccups, which were really starting to hurt my tummy. Thankfully it was a short journey, but there is nothing edifying about being driven back to school after midnight in a boy's bathrobe by a matron who drives a smarter car than your own mother.

As we turned into my school's car park, I could see the silhouette of Sister Constance standing on the entrance porch, and I could tell from her expression that she was not her usual composed, meditative self. Shame over my behaviour gave way to fear of what my punishment would be.

Kate had to come around and virtually drag me out of the car, I was so frozen with fear.

'Thank you, Mrs Denning, I'll take the matter from here,' Sister Constance assured her. 'It was very good of you to bring her back.'

'Not at all, and please, Sister, call me Kate,' she replied sweetly as she walked back towards her car.

'I'm soooo sorry, Sister,' I began in my most remorseful voice.

'We'll discuss what's to be done about this matter when your mother arrives in the morning,' was Sister's curt reply.

'When my mother arrives? But she works.'

'I called her as soon as Mrs Denning called me. You are lucky that you were discovered by Mrs Denning, a most understanding young woman. I can't bear to think of the scandal should one of the masters have found you. Nonetheless, it was still my responsibility to call your mother. She will be here for a nine o'clock meeting.'

Gulp. 'What did she say?'

But Sister wasn't to be drawn, and merely escorted me to my dorm. Her silence was far worse than if she'd scolded me.

I crept into my room, planning to collect my pyjamas and change in the en suite, but I fell foul of Star, who was stretched out on my floor.

'What happened?' demanded Star excitedly, turning on her torch.

I wasn't in the mood to discuss my evening of disaster, even with my best friend, but Star isn't the sort of girl to let things drop. 'Let's see, I climbed up the wrong wall, where I was discovered by Malcolm clinging to the wisteria outside his room. He said I could dry my clothes in his room, so it was really lucky I wore my matching Snoopy –'

Star grabbed me round the shoulders. 'Wait? You don't mean Malcolm McHamish, the filmmaker?'

'I don't know. He's an Eades boy in the Lower Sixth. Anyway so he offers me champagne. And then Portia's brother walks in, followed by Billy, followed by –'

'I sent Billy to look for you,' Portia whispered from her bed.

'Thanks, well, he found me and my Snoopy underwear drying on Malcolm's radiator and then –'

'Is Malcolm really, really fit with red hair?' Star probed.

'I think the two are mutually exclusive actually, darling,' Honey waded in.

'You're just jealous,' Star snapped back.

'You keep telling yourself that, Ginga features!' Honey replied nastily, referring to Star's own red hair.

I couldn't believe everyone kept interrupting me! How many of them had braved the wisteria of Eades in the pouring rain and ended up busted by a matron called Kate who drives like a lunatic? None, that's how many. Also, I could smell the delicious aroma of pizza. How could they have ordered pizza while I was drying my underwear in a strange boy's room? While I was virtually choking to death on champagne they should have been biting their nails with worry, not munching on a delicious illicit pizza.

'Look, doesn't anyone actually want to hear what happened?' I almost yelled. 'Otherwise I'm going to get into my pyjamas and go to bed,' I told them sulkily.

'Sorry, darling,' Star whispered. 'Keep going, I won't interrupt again, promise.'

'Right, so the matron caught me naked, well semi-naked. I was wearing Malcolm's robe − and yes, he does have red hair − and then Freds walked in.'

'OMG! What did he say?' Star asked.

'*Shhhhh!*' Portia hushed. 'Let her finish.'

'Not much. Something like, "I don't believe this," and then he walked off in a strop.'

'Shit,' Star said simply.

'I know. Can you imagine? There I was, sitting on Malcolm's bed, in Malcolm's robe, knocking back champagne. Anyway, I chased after him, which is when I ran into Kate.'

'Kate?'

'Oh yes, Kate's their matron, only she didn't look or act a bit matronly. I mean, Malcolm was standing right in front of her smoking and drinking, and she didn't do anything. Can you imagine!'

'All boys' schools are like that, darling. They treat them like grown men,' Portia explained. 'Whenever we go to Eades boating day, all the boys just wander around drinking and smoking, and when any of the beaks tell them to stop drinking they just say "Yes, sir" and carry on.'

Honey giggled. 'I think it's quite funny, actually.'

'What?'

'You being caught naked in another boy's room, darling,' she replied. 'I think it's hilarious, in fact. Freddie will never take you back now.'

'She's not a package,' Star snapped at her before turning to me. 'So anyway, what did this Kate woman say to you then?'

'Nothing. She grabbed me by the robe, took me down to her office, called Sister, drove me back here and that was it.'

'And what did Sister say?' asked Portia.

'She told me there will be a meeting with my mother tomorrow. I'm probably going to get expelled.'

'Why didn't you mace her?' Honey asked. 'Then you could have run off back to school and no one would have been the wiser.'

'Oh yes, I should have maced her,' I agreed sarcastically.

Star sneered, 'And quite probably gone to jail. So anyway, what did Malcolm say?'

'Does it actually matter what Malcolm said or didn't say?' I replied hotly. I was getting quite cross now with the way Star was obsessing over this Malcolm. 'He didn't say much, and I can't be bothered remembering. In fact, I partly blame him for all this. If he hadn't invited me in, urged me to take off my clothes, dry them on his radiator and drink champagne, I wouldn't be in this mess! Look,' I added, pausing mid-rant. 'Sorry, but I'm tired, hungry and upset. I just want to go to bed. Not that I'll be able to sleep. Sarah will probably make me move to Clapham with her.'

'I'm sure Sister won't be *that* horrible,' Star assured me confidently.

'Just say you ran away because you were upset about Sarah leaving Bob and coming from a broken home, darling. Nuns hate broken homes,' Honey suggested. 'You could hint that they abuse you; that's bound to get you sympathy.'

Why did everyone keep saying I came from a broken home! 'I don't come from a broken home!' I snapped.

'OK, OK, chill. God, I was only trying to be nice, darling,' Honey said crossly. 'It will tear at Sister's heartstrings, that's all. Think about it. She's let Georgina get away with loads since her father married Koo-Koo.'

'That's completely different,' I argued. 'Bob and Sarah will sort things out. I mean, they –'

'Hang on, Calypso,' Star interrupted just as I began to feel uncertain of my argument. 'As much as I hate to agree with Honey,' Star said, 'she has a point. Sarah and Bob are having problems, and I honestly don't think Sister will want to make things any tougher on Sarah or you. Just relax for now. You're upset and need some sleep. Things always seem better in the morning,' she assured me, giving me a hug.

I felt tears banking up behind my eyes as I hugged her back. 'Sorry if I was grumpy with you, and thanks for waiting up for me.'

'Don't be mad, we had fun. Just get some sleep. I'll see you at breakfast. Sweet dreams.'

'Night,' I replied.

'Night,' added Portia as Star left.

'At last,' groaned Honey, punching her pillow. 'Only children! They're always sooo selfish.' She sighed heavily.

If I wasn't so tired and emotional I would have laughed.

'Are you OK, Calypso?' Portia asked gently as I crept into the en suite to clean my teeth.

'Fine. I have to change,' I told her. I was too upset to talk.

'I ordered a pizza for you while you were out in case you were hungry when you got back. I noticed you didn't eat at supper. It's a small Hawaiian; the box is on your bed. It's probably cold now.'

I was soooo touched – and starving after my night of high drama – that I almost threw myself on her and cuddled her.

As it was, I changed into my Hello Kitty PJs and consumed the cold pizza in the solitude of the bathroom so I wouldn't disturb Honey. It was bliss.

FIFTEEN

The Quality of Mercy is Not Strained – It's Drained

Ravaging the pizza pretty much sorted me out hunger-wise and even calmed me down enough to get to sleep. Waking up was another matter. I never thought I'd say it, but I actually missed Miss Cribb's little gong, which she used to bang millimetres from our ears until we woke up in Year Ten.

Miss Cribb's torture-by-gong seemed mild in comparison to Miss Bibsmore's stick. 'Oi, Miss Kelly. Time to git up,' she insisted, prodding at my ribs.

Even when I eventually darted out of bed, she managed a few more prods.

'All right!' I yelled. 'I'm up, I'm up!' I told her, dodging the stick as I struggled into my gown and slippers.

'Well, be that as it may, I'm in the rhythm now and prod I will until you is in that bathroom making yerself presentable!'

'Fine!' I yelled back as I dived into the en suite, locking the door behind me. My previous night's activities at Eades had left me looking like a drug-rehab patient. After a quick splash of water on my face, a flash brush of my teeth, I pulled my hairbrush through my hair and climbed into my uniform. By the time I ran past a mirror it was too late to do anything about my hideous, frizzy, acid-rain hair. Apply the lip-gloss though I might, nothing was going to improve my confidence level that morning.

Everyone was really lovely to me in the ref at breakfast. Word was out that I had broken the fortress of Eades – even amongst the Year Sevens who worshipped anyone who had even pulled a boy – let alone entered the holy kingdom of fit boys.

Even Honey was sweet to me, offering me her croissant, which she'd dropped on the floor. She brushed it on my uniform before passing it to me faux kindly. 'Darling, you must be famished after last night's exertions,' she sympathised, rolling her eyes and flicking her beautiful hair – which only served to make me feel even more hideous. 'And I adore this American Tramp look you're going for this morning, it's soooo you.'

'Thanks,' I said, immune to anything Honey might care to throw at me. 'I look like a train wreck,' I told her, accepting the extra croissant even though I wasn't going to eat it. I wasn't that hungry thanks to Portia's thoughtfulness the night before.

Honey leaned in closer and whispered, 'Only, don't mention where you got that mace, darling, will you? If you do, you'll appreciate that I'll have to tell Daddy you lied, and I'd hate to give evidence against you in court. It would tear my heart in two.'

'What are you talking about?' I asked, having forgotten all about the mace, which was still in the pocket of Malcolm's robe in my room along with my phone.

'Well, sweetie darling, it would be libellous were you to mention my name to Sister Constance regarding the mace.' She pointed to her heart and looked at me with faux concern. 'I couldn't bear to visit you in Old Choky, darling.'

Indie gave her a poke in the ribs similar to the pokes Miss Bibsmore had rained down on me with her stick earlier.

'Ouch!' Honey screamed, but everyone ignored her, apart from Indie's security guys, who flinched as if desperate for the opportunity to shoot Honey.

'Libel is when you write it down, you illiterate chav,' Indie pointed out.

Star giggled and had to spit out her mouthful of hot chocolate before she snorted it up her nose. Then the bell rang and we all had to run off for room inspection, registration, chapel – and in my case the dreaded interview with Sister and Sarah.

'Is it true you were found naked in Prince Freddie's room?' A gaggle of tiny little Year Sevens asked – wide-eyed with awe as we made our way out towards registration later on.

'Yes,' Star told them, but all the good humour in the world couldn't stop the inevitable confrontation awaiting me in Sister's office.

Sarah was waiting on the wooden bench outside Sister's office dressed in the same pink Chanel suit she'd worn on Sunday. Her face was ashen, though, and her hair looked as dishevelled as my own.

'So, here we are, then, Calypso,' she said sternly. 'I really am at a loss as to what to say.'

'Yes, but I can explain, Sarah. Honestly, it isn't as bad as it seems.'

'I think you might find it's worse,' she told me ominously, looking miserably down at her hands. She had a quiver in her voice. 'Breaking into a boys' school. And naked? Oh, Calypso, what were you thinking?'

'I *wasn't* naked,' I told her outraged. 'At least not at first!' I blurted.

Unsurprisingly, this didn't mollify the madre. By the time Sister called 'Come!' Sarah looked on the verge of tears.

As usual, Sister was in silent meditation under a life-size statue of Christ that looked down on us from the crucifix above her chair. Her hands formed a steeple on the desk while her lips moved silently in prayer. Sarah and I waited for an invitation to be seated.

'Thank you for coming, Mrs Kelly. Please be seated,' Sister Constance said eventually, her voice laden with doom.

'Before you speak, Sister, I think there are mitigating circumstances in this case which you should know about,' Sarah began.

Sister shot her a warning look. 'Before *anyone* speaks,

Mrs Kelly, I intend to pray for guidance from the Lord God, Our Father, in the handling of this matter, thank you.'

So, we all set off on a decade of the rosary, and I promise you I've never prayed so fervently in my life. When Sister spoke again it was to explain that she felt inclined to suspend me for the duration of term.

Sarah looked at her furiously. She rose out of her chair and loomed – yes loomed (which isn't as hard as you might think for an abnormally tall woman in heels) over Sister's ancient oak desk.

I shrank into my chair.

'Suspend?' Sarah spat out the word as if it were akin to 'murder'. 'After everything this poor child from a broken home has endured?' She pointed to me. I crumpled up into the chair even further and began a slow slither to the floor.

Sister leaned over her desk, presumably curious as to what I was up to.

Sarah was oblivious to all as she tore strips off our head nun. 'I am disappointed in you, Sister,' she railed. 'Disappointed with a capital "D"! With her father in Los Angeles immersed in his own self-centred madness, her mother struggling to pay her fees while dealing with an emotionally-trying time. Just imagine what it's done to this poor child? Have you no soul, Sister?' she demanded. 'Have you no mercy?'

Sister replied calmly and softly, 'We all have souls, Mrs Kelly. Even girls such as your daughter, who run drunk and naked around Eades, have souls.'

'I didn't run naked around Eades and I wasn't drunk. I just

had the hiccups, that's all!' I cried out, but they both ignored me – partly because I was now crumpled on the floor.

'Well, then, Sister Constance. Where's your quality of mercy? Is it strained?' Sarah demanded to know. Sarah likes to paraphrase Shakespeare. It was usually a sign that she had dug herself into her argument and had no exit strategy in place. This was going to be a long and upsetting morning. The upside was I was missing Greek; the downside was Sarah's speech would no doubt end in my expulsion.

Sister tried to interject at various points, but Sarah waved her away dismissively. 'It beggars the belief of any right-thinking, moral person that you, a woman who has supposedly devoted yourself to the spiritual care of young ladies, can toss this poor child from a broken home on to the scrap heap of life to fend for herself while her mother is struggling to find her way in a new country and her father is on another continent, immersed in his bloody Big One!'

'Sit down, Mrs Kelly,' Sister commanded authoritatively.

Sarah obeyed, stunned I guess by Sister's transformation from earnest nun to terrifying draped woman. 'Now, get off the floor Miss Kelly. That is no place for a girl of Saint Augustine's to repose.'

'Yes, Sister,' Sarah and I chimed as I clambered back on to my chair.

'Now, as I said before your well-intentioned interruption, Mrs Kelly, my *inclination* is to suspend Calypso for the duration of the term. But one does not always give in to one's inclinations, does one?'

Sarah and I shook our heads fervently.

'So, as this is Calypso's GCSE year and her record, up until now, has been relatively blemish-free, I am prepared to be lenient. Taking in the circumstances of your parents' marital breakup and your mother's, erm, breakdown, Calypso, I am prepared to suspend your sentence and leave it as a weekend gating for now. However, and I mean this, so listen very carefully . . .'

Sarah and I both strained our ears to hear.

'Should you ever pull a stunt like this again, I warn you, I will not hesitate to give way to my inclinations and suspend you, GCSEs or not. Understood?'

'Oh, Sister. Thank you for showing such mercy,' Sarah grovelled shamelessly. 'Calypso learned a very valuable lesson and I'm sure she's very sorry and grateful for your leniency.'

I was not so grovelly or shameless, though. 'Hang on a minute, Sister. You haven't even asked me my side of the story. This is soooo unfair. I was only at Eades because Freds wouldn't take my calls and I had to say sorry about, well, never mind about what, but since when has saying sorry been a crime?' I blurted.

Sister looked down at her lap.

Sarah jabbed me in the ribs. 'Ouch!' I yelped. Was this Jab Calypso In The Ribs Day or something? 'I was only wearing Malcolm's robe because my own clothes were wet.'

'I think, Calypso, you have said and done quite enough,' said Sister.

I scowled at her. Sarah patted my shoulder. 'There, there,

Calypso, you've been under a lot of strain lately,' she soothed as if I were some sort of lunatic.

I shrugged her off. 'Besides, you can't gate me this weekend. I've got the tournament! Mr Wellend says people are watching me. Spies and BNFA-type people. He'll go bonkers.'

Sarah mouthed the word 'shut up' at me.

Sister looked up. 'The gating was not a suggestion, Miss Kelly. You are gated, young lady, tournament or no tournament,' Sister said in a tone of voice that brooked no further argument.

'But Bell End, he'll have my guts for garters,' I blurted.

'Have you heard the expression, "Skating on thin ice"?' Sister asked me.

I nodded.

'How about the expression "When you're in a hole, stop digging"?'

I nodded again.

'Well, Madam, you are skating on thin ice and digging one crater of a hole for yourself. As part of your gating you will also lose all mobile phone privileges for a week.'

'But you can't do that, it's against – something or other!' I shrieked. 'It's against European Law and violates my human rights under the, erm, Belgium Convention!' I hazarded.

Sister rose and glared. 'For the sake of your future here at Saint Augustine's School for Young Ladies, Calypso, I am terminating this meeting before you jeopardise the lenient punishment the Lord has guided me to grant you. Good morning, Mrs Kelly.'

And with that, Sister Constance swept out of her office, taking my future with her.

I looked up at our Lord on his cross. 'So that's what you call lenient, is it, oh Lord of Mercy?' I asked sarcastically.

'I've been fired,' Sarah said, quietly.

'Fired?'

'Yes, they're cutting back.'

I put my arm about her as if I were one of those rock-solid-type daughters as opposed to the dependent, emotionally-needy daughter I really was. 'You're madly talented, Sarah, you'll be snapped up before you can say –'

'Snappy dialogue.'

'Exactly, snappy dialogue,' I agreed.

'No, that's why they fired me. They said I was too scripted, that my dialogue wasn't snappy enough.'

'Idiots,' I said.

We sat there for a bit. I stroked Sarah's back and she made a brave, resigned face. I didn't ask anything tricky about who'd pay my fees or how she'd afford the house or, well, anything that might yield an answer that might make me feel even worse.

But Sarah must have sensed the thoughts chasing through my mind because she said, 'I've got some savings; they will hold us for a few months, but after that –'

'And I might win the essay competition. You never know.'

Sarah smiled. 'You're everything to me, you know that, don't you, Calypso?'

I nodded as I squeezed her hand. 'I know. And, erm,

sorry about the, you know, going to Eades thing.'

'Oh, darling Calypso, I don't mind about that, really. I did it myself more times than I care to remember. Do you really think I'd be cross with you about a streak through Eades?'

I didn't get a chance to tell her 'yes' because the bell for the next class rang, so I had to leg it to get my books for English.

SIXTEEN

The Extreme Trauma
of Privilege

'Miss Kelly,' said Ms Topler as I wandered into class all of one minute late.

'Yes, Miss?'

'Come and see me after class, please.'

This was soooo typical. As if I didn't have enough on my plate, now Ms Topler wanted to give me a blue. I hated teachers.

I slumped into a chair next to Star. 'So what did Sister say?' she whispered.

'No mobile phone for a week and a gating.'

'That's not too bad.'

'Are you mad? How can I call Freddie to explain about being virtually naked in Malcolm's room? And I won't get to go to the fencing tournament with Portia and attract the attention of the spies and scouts.'

'What spies and scouts? You're being paranoid. Bell End is clearly a loon. There *are* no spies and scouts, Calypso, apart from in his deranged imagination,' Star assured me.

'I will not have chatting in my class, thank you, Star and Calypso,' Ms Topler called out.

'No, Ms Topler,' I answered. 'Star was just showing me what I missed.'

'You haven't missed anything, as Star well knows,' Ms Topler snapped. 'Now, open up your copies of *Sons and Lovers*. Miss Castle Orpington, could you please begin the fourth chapter for us.'

And so the lesson dragged and droned on. I almost fell asleep; in fact I must have dozed off a bit because the next thing I heard was the bell.

I grabbed my books and pencil case and started to make my way out in the shuffle of girls, but Ms Topler hadn't forgotten.

'Miss Kelly, I believe I asked you to stay back,' she called out to me.

'Oh, sorry, Ms Topler, my mind was on the incandescence of D.H. Lawrence.'

She rolled her eyes. 'Enough, Calypso. You are a talented pupil but a less talented fibber. Work on your strengths rather than your weaknesses.'

'Yes, Ms Topler.'

'Now take a seat while I get something that I hope might interest you.'

I sat down in a chair by the window and looked out over Puller's Wood at the golden carpet of fallen leaves. The bare branches looked so forlorn – a bit like I felt. Ms Topler handed me a pamphlet. The same pamphlet Star had given me about the essay competition.

'I've given these entries out to the Year Tens and below,

as the competition is limited to the Under Fifteens. You don't turn fifteen until after the end of this term, do you, though, Miss Kelly?'

'No,' I replied.

Ms Topler sat on the seat beside me, which meant I could smell her perfume, Red Door by Elizabeth Arden. I tried not to choke on the strong fumes and pretended to pay attention. 'I knew it. Don't you see what this means?' she asked excitedly.

'That I don't get any proper birthday presents because my birthday is only days away from Christmas.'

'Don't be silly. It's just that people try to get you one big present,' she said, patting my arm.

'I think we both know that's a big lie,' I told her.

'Yes, perhaps it is. My birthday is on the twenty-fourth of December.'

'It sucks, doesn't it?' I blurted before I could help myself.

'Yes, it does rather,' agreed my teacher. 'But what doesn't suck is that your late birthday makes you eligible to enter the competition and, while I don't want to get your hopes up *too* high, I certainly think you have the ability to win this – if you put your heart and soul into it.'

I turned the pamphlet around in my hands and realised that my gating might give me the opportunity to work on the essay. 'Thank you, Ms Topler, but do you really think my pathetic sufferings such as they are can compete with the other applicants?'

'Miss Kelly, you can't measure suffering. And besides, this is a writing competition. The judges will be judging you on how well you express your suffering, not on what your suffering has been.' She was looking into my eyes like a hypnotist.

'I guess,' I agreed as I began to realise that it was all about the writing, not the suffering. I'd been looking at it the wrong way. OK, so my life had been a bed of roses compared to some, but there is a universality about suffering, and Bob is always saying that being a successful writer is about the ability to communicate the personal in the universal.

'Just consider this. Knowing all the other things you have on your plate, I wouldn't suggest this essay competition if I didn't think you had a real chance. You have a rare talent, Miss Kelly. This could be your opportunity to show the country, and at the very least to explore your potential.'

'Thank you, Ms Topler,' I said, smiling at her hopeful face.

'So you'll try it?'

'I'll give it my best shot.'

And then Ms Topler did something so unexpected it toppled me – quite literally to the ground. She slapped me really hard on the back and said, 'That's my girl!' And then she laughed and laughed and said, 'One big present indeed. You're absolutely right, Miss Kelly. It sucks.'

So now it was official. I was entering an autobiographical writing competition which would depict my suffering in all its middle-class glumness.

SEVENTEEN

Bell End's Sacred Sabre

I know my mobile had been confiscated, but there is e-mail, after all. Bob and Sarah were addicted to it. I wrote to Freddie trying to explain why I had tried to patch things up with him in a dressing gown in Malcolm's room, but he didn't reply.

Fine, *he* could sulk if he wanted to, but I was damned if I wasn't going to tell Bob what I thought of him.

Dear Bob,

I hope you are very pleased with yourself! Sarah has now lost her job thanks to you. I can't believe that a father of mine could be so cold and allow a woman to whom he once vowed to forsake above all others (including Big Ones) to end up on the scrap heap of life. You and your creative endeavours have been the downfall of this family. From this day forth I shall name you, well, I don't know what yet, but when I think of it, you can be certain it will make you sorry you were ever born. Also, now that poor Sarah has lost her job, how can she pay my fees and support herself? And her self-esteem is in ruins. And she's seeing a therapist called Bunny – well, phoning her, because this

Bunny creature lives in LA. Anyway, it's all a Big Mess and it's all
your fault. And I hate you. And I've just had a gating.
    From your daughter Calypso
    PS: Note the lack of xxx's!!!

Talk about living at his laptop! His response came roaring
back as defiant as a teenage girl's! And if, like me, you were
expecting an e-mail of remorse, a few lines of his heartfelt
shame or an explanation for driving Sarah to England – or
a grovelling plea for me to forgive him – you'll be disappointed.

    Dearest Daughter,
    Sarah has spoken to me of your naked romp around the
dormitory rooms of Eades! Please explain immediately.
    Your loving father, Bob
    NB: xxxxxxxxxxxxxxxxxxxxxxxxxxxxxxxxxxxxxxxxxxxxxx

How dare he!

    Dear 'Daddy', [I replied, righteous steam coming out of
my ears.]
    Bugger off. I hate you and everything you stand for and
shan't write to you again. Consider yourself persona non
grata.
    C
    PS: I soooo wasn't naked!

Since she moved to England, Sarah had been sending me

little letters written on art gallery postcards, which I have
lovingly pinned to my pin board.

'How could Bob let a woman like her slip through his
fingers?' Star asked as postcard after postcard arrived. The
rest of the time she went on and on about the competition.
'You are soooo winning that competition! I just know it.'

It was with some trepidation that I entered the salle,
knowing I would have to tell Bell End that I wouldn't be
attending the tournament on Saturday.

He bounded over like a spaniel in white breeches to
greet me. 'Here she is!' he cried, clapping his hands with
glee. Clearly no one had told him about my gating.

Portia joined him half-heartedly because word had
spread through school already about my punishment.
There was even a rather clever haiku in the downstairs loos
about my Eades escapades, followed by another about my
punishment.

'That's right, big round of applause, Portia. Crank it up
there.'

It was soooo embarrassing. Seriously – he was standing on
a block with his loud inhaler while the 'Ride of the Valkyries'
played on a gramophone in the corner of the room.

'Take a bow, Kelly! You little champ.'

'Erm, Mr Wellend, I actually need to talk to you.'

'Plenty of time for talk after class, Kelly. Now how about
you climb up on my shoulders for a victory run around the
school, eh? Let's show them what we're made of, eh, Kelly,
eh!'

So that was that. What was I to say? He'd already bent

down, so I climbed up on to his shoulders and we ran through the school, into classrooms and bedrooms, creating havoc and madness, especially in the convent. Sister Regina, who was soooo obviously expecting us, had a big spread of Battenberg cakes and tea set out for Portia, Bell End and myself. The nuns were only allowed to eat the cucumber sandwiches, and a very sulky atmosphere prevailed.

'We're all very proud of you, Calypso,' they told me at one time or another, usually when I passed them a piece of illicit Battenberg cake.

When we arrived back in the salle, I couldn't put my moment of truth off any longer, though.

'Mr Wellend, I have to tell you something.'

He ruffled my hair affectionately.

'You can tell me anything, Kelly, anything. As long as you distinguish yourself at the Brighton Open on Saturday that is, ha-ha-ha.'

'Oh! Well, that's it, you see. I've been g-g-g-g-g-gated.'

Bell End thwacked me on the back – and really hard too. 'What was that? A piece of cake going down the wrong way? Oh yes, mark my words, Kelly, Brighton will be where we really stick it to them. The scouts all gathered. The scene all set. It's going to be a bloodbath, my girl. And I, for one, can't wait. So without further ado, I hereby present you with this blade of death that I distinguished myself with all those years ago at the Olympics.'

That was when he passed me a sabre, which I accepted. Well, better in my hands than his, was my reasoning. At least I'd be armed if he went crazy upon hearing the news that I really wasn't going to Brighton on Saturday. I studied the weapon, which was slightly rusty, and noted with some amusement that it had the words 'KILL, SLAY, MAIM' scratched childishly into the guard.

'That's really kind, Mr Wellend. I'll treasure it.'

'Steady up there, Kelly. You can't keep it, you idiot. I won silver with that.' He snatched it back crossly. I was just showing you, yer brainless girl. What kind of fool would give a weapon like this away to an untried schoolgirl. I barely know you, child.'

'Oh, sorry, my mistake, Mr Wellend, but it does bring me to the thing I had to tell you actually, about my, erm, gating on Saturday, see.'

Bell End's face started to go a nasty shade of purple. 'Gated? What do you mean gated? Sister can't gate you on Saturday. We've got the tournament!'

I was really regretting giving him his sabre back so quickly. 'Yes, that's what I said when Sister Constance gated me, funnily enough.' I laughed as best I could. 'And she took my mobile privileges off me, which I think is madly unfair and draconian, for supposedly running half-naked around Eades and drinking a bit of champagne, but honestly –'

'What would you want to be drinking champagne and running around naked for when you've got the Nationals coming up?' Bell End demanded hotly. 'You should be prac-tising your footwork, Kelly.'

'I wasn't properly naked, Mr Wellend. I mean, I was wearing a robe.'

'I'm not interested in your nudity, but what's robes got to

do with it? You're not Harry bloody Potter, girl. Robes? What were you wearing robes for? What's a sabreur want with robes?' Bell End demanded hotly.

Portia, who had been standing nearby waiting for the fireworks, gave him a pat on the back. 'She'll still be at the Regionals sir, and *I'll* be coming on Saturday.'

'You're a good little fencer, Briggs,' Bell End turned to her seemingly composed momentarily. 'But the scouts! The BNFA spies? What am I to tell them? I've set my trap, Briggs! Planned every intricate move to lure them into my web. Kelly! What have you done to me?' he cried out like a man in true pain.

'Well, see, sir, the thing is, I was looking for my boyfriend to say sorry because –'

'I don't care if you were looking for the Holy Grail, you stupid girl. They don't put you on the National Team because you've chased down a spineless boyfriend in a robe. What kind of nancy boy has you playing hide-and-seek with him, anyway?'

'Erm, Prince Freddie, sir.'

Bell End shook his head. 'I blame those romantic novels they feed you. Prince bloody Freddie, indeed! I bet it was that Eades fencing master set the whole thing up. Entrapment, that's what it is. I'll be complaining to the BNFA, I will. Entrapment.'

'But can't Calypso meet the scouts and, erm, spies at the Regionals?' Portia suggested gently.

Bell End bent his sword into the piste in fury. 'No, she bloody can't! These men don't have memories. Here today, gone tomorrow. No!' With that he threw his prized sabre down the piste.

'Get out of my sight, Kelly. You've let me down. You've let everyone down. My plan to make you an Olympian, blown away like a house of straw. Spineless, big girl's blouse, that's all you are. Robes! Git out of my sight. Out, I say!'

I began to run out of the salle, tears streaming down my face.

Then Bell End shouted, 'Where do you think you're going, Kelly?'

I turned. 'Out of your sight, Bell End, I mean, Mr Wellend,' I whimpered.

He slapped his forehead like a truly frustrated man. 'I don't believe this, lily-livered girls. Git back in here.' He pointed to the floor. 'Drop and give me twenty, now.'

I looked at Portia. Portia shrugged.

'Are you deaf as well as stupid, Kelly? Drop, both of you. Yes, you too, Briggs. I daresay they'd have you in a robe as well if you'd won the tournament. Give me twenty.'

So drop we did and gave him twenty press-ups.

That was how my week of fencing continued. Bell End ranting about his scout ruse being ruined followed by punishing exercises and rants about 'bloody robes'. I don't think Portia was too impressed with me for bringing the wrath of Bell End down on us, either.

EIGHTEEN

The Return of Octavia

B ell End's mood towards me didn't improve over the rest of the week. His sacred sabre didn't appear again, which I took as significant. Nor did the rain let up. Freddie continued to reject all my calls, which I now had to make from a call box that was a half-mile trek in the rain from the dorm. He also ignored all my e-mails. On the up side, I really did try and pull my tights up when it came to my studies and handed in an outstanding Greek translation, which I was pretty sure would garner me an A, or a B, at least. Definitely a C anyway.

Sarah e-mailed me every day, but her attempt at sounding upbeat and her overuse of the word 'super' didn't fool me. She was going on loads of interviews and her agent was 'confident'. I wished I were as confident as this agent.

Portia had already left for the tournament by the time I woke up on Saturday. It was pissing down with rain still, and breakfast was only stale cereal and powdered milk due to some transport strike. Star and Indie decided to hang with me rather than go into Windsor with everyone else, which was really sweet of them, especially because I knew how much Star wanted to see Kev.

The truth was, as kind as it was of Star to stay with me, I would have rather been on my own and worked on my essay. Having overcome my earlier reservations, I was now keen to get cracking on the essay competition.

After breakfast, I lay on my bed and thought about what I would write. Three thousand words of personal life-changing trauma seemed a lot for an almost-fifteen-year old. It's funny, but the more I thought about my life, the more sorrow I saw.

Being an American in an English girls' boarding school.

The misery that Bob's need to pursue his own creative endeavours had wrought on our family.

My concern for Sarah's loneliness and the sense of failure she felt.

How I felt about her leaving Bob to have her regressionary breakdown in London.

And then there was Freds, who wouldn't talk to me.

Oh, and let's not forget the toxic Honey, using me as her torture toy at every opportunity these past four years.

Slowly I began to see that there really was some class-A trauma going on in my life. In fact, would three thousand words be enough?

Honey, Clemmie and Arabella headed off to Windsor after lessons at one o'clock but Star and Indie charged into my room just as I was making some really serious break-throughs. I told them I was busy, but Star gave me a speech about solidarity and standing shoulder to shoulder with the suffering of the sisterhood or something Star-ish like that.

'I just know you'll win this writing competition, Calypso,' Indie said, displaying a confidence in me she really had no reason to have, given she'd only known me half a term.

'I told her what a genius you are with words,' Star explained.

'And I seriously love *The Nun*,' Indie added, referring to the magazine I'd set up in Year Ten. 'I'd love to hear what you've written so far,' she pleaded.

So I read them out what I'd written, giving a little cough to set the mood: 'Talk about random. This was the worst-case scenario in my long history of worst-case scenarios. But then, my entire life is a random series of worst-case scenarios. At fourteen you start to realise these things.' I looked around my audience and smiled hopefully.

'Go on,' Star urged, her eyes bright with anticipation.

'Erm, that's as far as I've got, actually,' I explained.

'Oh,' she said, *très* unimpressed. Then she rolled her eyes at me so I rolled mine back at her, then Indie rolled hers at both of us. I suspect we could have gone on like this until we had a fit or dislocated an eye, but we were interrupted by a tapping sound at the window.

'It's Kev!' cried Star, rushing over to open the window for her very wet boyfriend.

'And Malcolm,' I added, recognising that red thatch of hair even though it was plastered to his head.

'And Freds!' Indie yelped as the shame-faced grin of my

one and only true love lit up our dark little room. I didn't care how wet he was as he pulled me into his arms and snog-aged me into a state of bliss. When we drew breath he asked if I could ever forgive him for being such a paranoid idiot.

Malcolm tussled Fred's hair and grinned at me. 'The appropriate answer would be no, Calypso,' he advised. 'Oh, by the way, I brought you this,' he added passing me a miniature bottle of Veuve. 'And don't worry, I took the precaution of removing the straw for you already,' he teased.

I know I should have just been happy that Freds had forgiven me, but I couldn't help wondering what had changed his mind. I hoped it was sleepless night upon sleepless night remembering our kisses that had made him realise he couldn't live without me. But I suspected Malcolm might have had something to do with it.

Speaking of Malcolm, I couldn't help notice the way Indie was staring at him, like a huntress eyeing up her prey. Freddie had his arms around me still, and I nuzzled his neck the way Kev was nuzzling Star's.

Star pulled away, though. 'I'm a huge fan of your work, Malcolm,' she gushed.

'Cheers, and you are?'

'Sorry,' I said. 'This is Star and this is Indie and –' but Indie took it from there.

'Star's told me *all* about your films, especially *Trousers in Cannes*. I can't wait to see it,' she practically gushed. 'I love experimental silent film. Voices are soooo overrated.'

'You haven't been advertising again, have you,

McHamish?' Freddie teased, giving Malcolm a friendly shove (right in the direction of Indie, I noted).

'How did you know we'd be here?' I asked Freds. 'I was meant to be in Brighton today.'

'Yaah, but you're not. Thanks to me,' Freddie replied, looking shame-faced again. 'Kev told me. I'm really sorry about how I reacted last week. I guess I was just so shocked, seeing you there on McHamish's bed.'

'He was particularly pissed off about your rather fetching Snoopy bra and knickers on my radiator,' Malcolm ribbed.

Freddie went red.

'Oh, I know. It must have looked terrible, what with my trackie bums and –'

Star slashed her hand across her neck, indicating now would be a perfect opportunity for me to shut up.

'I wasn't aware they did matching Snoopy lingerie,' Malcolm added unhelpfully. 'Cute little ensemble, Pyke,' he explained to Kev. 'You see, they had little Woodstocks on them and everything. Very arty. I'm not normally a lingerie man myself, but personally I've always felt that Woodstock was way underrated. He carried that cartoon strip as far as I can tell.'

I glared at him.

'Oh, by the way, Calypso,' he continued unabashed. 'Could I grab my robe back?'

'Sure, it's hanging on the back of the en suite door there,' I told him before turning back to Freds. 'But I only came to Eades to see you, Freds. I didn't even know Malcolm then and I was just soooo wet and lost and well –'

Freddie put his hands up in resignation. 'I know, mea culpa, mea culpa, McHamish told all. The vine, the rain, the cold, but Calypso we need to get something straight.'

'Yes?'

'I get pissed off when you do these totally random, unexpected, inexplicable, illogical things. It's just confusing and makes me feel, well, insecure, I suppose.'

'How can you be insecure, Freds, when you've got a girl who's prepared to brave that wisteria bush in the rain. Tomkins broke his collarbone trying that stunt, remember,' Malcolm pointed out.

I was almost swooning, though, at the idea that I had the capacity to make an HRH *insecure*. Sorry, but how hot is that?

Star, who'd been towelling off Kev's hair, waded in to my defence. She's never had much time for Freds and wasn't going to let him off his sulk that easily. 'She was only looking for you! It's a wonder she didn't catch pneumonia and die. If it weren't for Malcolm helping her out, we might all be at her funeral now, not listening to you whine about how insecure you are.' She may as well have added 'You stuck up royal high horse,' given the tone she used.

Freds responded by going red and wiping his hand through his own dripping wet hair. 'I've been a bit of a shit, haven't I?'

I can't tell you how adorable he looked. I wanted to give him a towel and dry him off like Star had Kev, but I got the feeling Star would flip out if I did.

'Yes, you are a shit,' Star told him crossly. 'A royal bloody shit, now get down on your knees and apologise to all of us. To Calypso, for believing the worst of her. Then you can apologise to Malcolm for not being more grateful to him for helping your girlfriend out. And last but not least, you can say sorry to Indie and me for having to put up with Calypso being so bloody miserable all week when she's got enough on her plate with her parents splitting up. Oh, and to Kev for being your mate and having to put up with your misplaced sense of grandeur twenty-four-seven. Insecure, my arse.'

Indie giggled, and I noticed Malcolm looking at her like a lovesick puppy.

Freddie wiped some raindrops off his face. God, he was fit. I really wished Star could see how lovely he was, which I bet she would if she got to know him properly. 'Erm, can we go somewhere on our own for a chat?' he asked me quietly.

After checking whether Star had heard, I nodded, too happy to trust myself to speak. Star was busily dabbing Kev's nose with the towel.

'Calypso and I are just going to nip into the bathroom for a chat,' he said looking straight at Star. 'Before I go I'd just like to say, to all of you, especially Calypso, obviously, who's the best girlfriend a boy could wish for . . .' Then, and this is true, I swear, he got down on his knees and arms out-stretched said, '. . . forgive me, ladies and McHamish and Kev, for I have done ye wrong.'

Malcolm gave him a gentle kick. 'Piss off, you idiot, you were always crap at drama.' And then everyone laughed –

even Star (well, she rolled her eyes and smiled) – and Freds and I went into the en suite for a quiet chat.

So there we were, his insecure Royal Highness and me. He sat on the loo and I sat on his lap, and after a nice bit of pulling, he took my chin in his hands and turned my head to his own. I was forced to look into his eyes, which always gives me this melted-chocolate feeling. 'I am sorry, Calypso.'

I nodded mutely, staring into the gorgeousity of his face.

'Oh shit, what kind of king will I make? I always seem to get the wrong end of the stick. And I didn't even think about what you must be going through with your parents separating. God, are you OK?'

I nodded. 'You know 'rents.'

'Yes, my parents are the ones responsible for the security dopes I'm always trying to shake.'

I giggled. 'I think you should count yourself lucky. Mine are just plain nuts.'

'Well, so are mine, but at least I let you meet mine. You, on the other hand, didn't want to subject your mother to the horror of me! How do you think I felt when you legged it down the lane? I presume you've told her all sorts of horrible lies about me.'

I went so red I thought my eyes would start bleeding. 'No, it wasn't you, it was her. Sarah's gone completely mad since she left Bob. She's started reverting. I couldn't subject you to that.'

'Reverting?'

'Regressing, you know, talking to me like I'm three, and, well, you don't want to hear about my problems.'

'See. This is what I'm talking about. You are maddening, Calypso. Of course I want to talk about your reverting mother. I want to talk about everything with you. But you're always sending me these mixed signals.'

'Me?'

'Yes, you. You're never doing what you're meant to be doing, never where you're meant to be, and you never even say what I think you're going to say. And after all that phone confusion rubbish before half-term, it's like mixed signal after mixed signal. I feel like I can never relax. I know loads of our problems were down to Honey, and we're over that but, despite Star's opinion of me, I actually do get insecure where you're concerned because you won't let me get to know you properly. You really are like Cinderella, disappearing every time I feel like we're getting close, and all I'm left with is a glass slipper that doesn't fit anyone else.'

Then he kissed me for a very, very, very long time. When we stopped I wiped a wet tentacle of hair from his forehead.

'You're not like any other girl I've ever met, Calypso. Apart from being madly stunning and adorable, you are the singularly most infuriatingly difficult girlfriend a boy ever had.'

I was about to kiss him again, but he pushed me away.

'No, I will not be distracted from my prepared speech,' he teased, laughingly. 'I've thought about this a lot while I've been sulking, and the truth is . . .' (he did a nervous throat-clearing thing) 'I love you, Calypso, and everything you do drives me crazy.'

Shocked didn't even come close to how I was feeling at

that moment, but before I could form an articulate sentence, we all heard the *tap, tap, tap* of Miss Bibsmore's stick coming down the corridor towards us. The duct tape must have fallen off her carpet-square silencer.

I grabbed Freds and dived out of the en suite. Star looked at me. Kev looked at Freds. Indie looked at Malcolm.

'She's going to come in here,' Star hissed, looking around at all of us, her eyes large saucers of terror.

I looked outside, where it had started to hail.

'They haven't got time to make it out,' I said, as Miss Bibsmore's stick could be heard outside our door.

'Here,' Star told the boys, chucking clothes from Honey's drawer at them in bundles and shoving them into the en suite.

She had no sooner slammed the door on them when Miss Bibsmore entered our room in her awkward little shuffle. 'I've brought you some sweets, Miss Kelly,' she said as she passed a bag of jelly beans over to me. 'I know this gating is difficult for you an' all, what with the fencing competition, but discipline is discipline.'

I heard noises coming from the en suite, and so I shook the packet of jelly beans loudly in the pathetic hope of drowning out the boy's racket and cried, 'Thank you, Miss Bibsmore, you're soooo sweet.'

Why were boys so loud, even when they are supposed to quiet? I had to keep rattling on. 'Yes, Miss Bibsmore. Thank you, Miss Bibsmore. That is sooo, kind, Miss Bibsmore,' I said, as loudly as I could without shouting.

Star and Indie joined in with 'Aren't you a duck, Miss Bibsmore! You are the best house mother ever! So kind. Poor Calypso. She just loves jelly beans.'

'All right, all right! I might be crippled, but I is not deaf! Leastways not last time I heard,' Miss Bibsmore cried, holding her hands over her ears.

The boys in the en suite began to giggle.

'What was that?' asked our house spinster. 'Have you got company?'

Indie dived to the rescue. 'Just a few chums from an upper year. They came down to, erm, help us with erm –'

'Some hard sums,' added Star. Talk about a lame excuse, normally Star is razor sharp when it comes to quick-thinking excuses.

'Their bathroom was blocked, so I said they could use mine,' I explained.

'Oh yes, well, very generous of you, Miss Kelly, I'm sure.' But she didn't look totally convinced.

Then the boys giggled even louder. Thanks, guys.

Placing one of her arthritic hands on the doorknob of the en suite, Miss Bibsmore demanded that the 'girls' show themselves. Please, please, please I thought, you *have* locked the door!

But they hadn't locked the door. Of course they hadn't done anything as sensible as that. What was I thinking? They were boys.

'Out you git,' Miss Bibsmore clucked, poking her stick into the en suite to hustle the boys out.

Malcolm, Freds, and Kevin wriggled out, deftly dodging

the blows of Miss Bibsmore's stick. Each had a towel wrapped around his head as a turban, each with a face smeared with make-up a three-year-old child would be proud of. Malcolm was wearing his robe, while Freds and Kevin were each dressed in Honey's trackie bums and hoodies. They looked like transvestites who hadn't quite found their way around the make-up counter yet. Malcolm had daubed body glitter all over his face.

'What are your names, girls?' Miss Bibsmore asked suspiciously, eyeing up my boyfriend and his friends.

'My name's Octavia,' Freds replied in a falsetto voice that could break glass.

'Oh, my darling girl,' Miss Bibsmore cried out, almost weeping with joy as she tossed her stick to the floor and threw her arms around my boyfriend (who loved me) with an abandon I'd never seen. 'You've come back, Octavia. I knew you would. The others said you'd gone and got your-self preggers. Oh, you dear, dear, dear girl.'

After that she began to cry. 'This little poppet here was like a daughter to me an' all.' She gave Fred's cheek a big pinch. 'Then one day some horrible boy from Eades pitched up here on a motorbike, mind, and took 'er off. Never saw her again.'

'Heavens,' said Indie, still transfixed by Malcolm, *avec* make-up and all. It was obvious she fancied him like mad.

'But I'm back now, Miss,' Freds squeaked. 'I've only dropped in for the day, though – the little tot needs me now.'

'Oh, so the rumours were true,' Miss Bibsmore

grumbled. 'But maybe that's for the best. A baby has clearly helped you to grow into a fine young woman, dear,' Miss Bibsmore said. 'Mind you, a girl with your looks and figure doesn't need all that muck on her face, in my opinion.' She patted Freds on the cheek.

'Seems like just yesterday, Miss,' Freds agreed, grinning stupidly.

'I could sit here and chat all day,' Miss Bibsmore said wistfully.

'Oh, please stay,' Malcolm begged in the most ridiculous attempt at sounding like a girl I'd ever heard. It took a lot of discipline not to grab Miss Bibsmore's stick and whack him with it, I can tell you. I don't know what he could have been thinking. Indie on the other hand seemed deeply impressed, as if Malcolm was some sort of really talented, god-like boy and not the fool he clearly was.

'No, girls, I just dropped in to see how poor Calypso was getting on, but I can see she's not short of a friend or two, and for that I'm pleased.' She beamed at the boys as well as at Star and Indie as she said this. 'No, unfortunately, I've promised the nuns a game of poker and I can't let *them* down now, can I?'

'Octavia' and friends shook their heads as if saddened to miss out on the company of our house mistress.

Miss Bibsmore opened her arms expansively. 'Well, then, give your Bibby a big hug, eh, Octavia? And next time I see you, I don't want to see all that muck on your face, eh?'

With that, our house mistress wrapped 'Octavia' in a big cuddle, said a tearful farewell and waved as she waddled off.

As the sound of her stick disappeared down the corridor, we all used pillows to smother our giggles.

'He's always popular with the old girls, is our Freds,' Malcolm teased.

Freds hit him with the pillow he'd been suffocating his laughter with and after that a pillow-and-duvet-and-any-thing-soft-we-could-lay-our-hands-on fight ensued.

Afterwards we kissed some more, but eventually the boys had to leave. Indie gave Malcolm a kiss, on the lips, when they were leaving, which of course meant a massive grilling from Star and me afterwards.

When Honey returned from Windsor later, she asked, 'Why is there make-up all over my pillow and duvet?'

But all we could do was laugh.

Nothing could spoil my high. Freds loved me!

NINETEEN

It's Your Love Life
or Your Life!

It's funny, but these last couple of terms – since meeting Freds – I never imagined it could be possible to survive life without a mobile phone. Who would have thought that there were ways of struggling through? Fred's visit helped because now I was no longer plagued by guilt that I was an inconsiderate, mean and selfish girlfriend. Also, Portia was letting me use her phone, so that was a lot easier than trekking to the public phone box, but it still wasn't the same without text messages to read and reread under the covers after lights out.

The real reason for my *joie de vivre*, though, was that Freds loved me.

Just to remind myself of this sublime fact I wrote it on my pencil case during double maths. When Star saw it, she thumped me with it over the head.

'Don't be such a lovesick puppy. You should be focusing on the essay competition,' she scolded.

'*Ow*,' I said, rubbing my head. 'I'm not going to have the

brains left to focus on anything at this rate if you keep thumping me.'

Actually, I had thrown myself into the task of writing my essay. It started off quite well too, with all that pathos about being an American and coming from Hollywood and being packed off to boarding school, where I was tortured by Honey – all the obviously tragic things like that. I changed Honey's name to Sweetie, but otherwise it was all true, just as the competition rules dictated.

But then, when I started on the part about my parents and their breakup, I began to feel that I might be showing Bob and Sarah in a rather poor light. Bob was coming across in the essay as this self-obsessed brute who put his stupid old Opus over and above his family, when clearly as a father and husband he should be loving us and earning money to support us. But what could I do with only three thousand words with which to depict my agony?

Sarah wasn't coming over too well in the essay, either. What with her regression issues, she was coming across as a bit of a spoiled child. I blamed the three thousand-word limit, which didn't allow me to explain how genuinely kind and generous she was. I began to ramble on about how in sickness and in health she always put me first, but that had made the essay too long, so I had to cut it out.

Eventually I showed what I'd written to Ms Topler.

Ms Topler and I have had our issues over the years. She thinks literature is Charlotte Brontë and other odd bores, whereas I think literature is Nancy Mitford. Come to think of it Nancy's best-selling book was a thinly veiled essay on her family. Then again, some of her relatives never spoke to her again after it was published.

The next day, Ms Topler collared me in the corridor on my way to chapel. She was rapturous in her praise. 'This is magnificent writing, Calypso. So real. So straight from the heart. So eloquent! Meaningful and simply dripping with pain.'

'So you don't think it might upset my parents . . . you know, all that talk of Bob's Big One and Sarah's self-interest?'

She laughed. 'Dear Miss Kelly, you are such a button. No, I don't think it reads as anything other than truly truthful and beautiful.'

'I mean, they are really kind people in their own mad way. But all parents are mad, aren't they?'

Ms Topler looked at me pityingly. 'Naturally you must cling to that delusion if it helps,' she replied, patting me on the head, but I heard her mutter, 'Poor, dear Calypso.'

'What's that supposed to mean?' I asked hotly.

'Nothing, dear, and you're right. I'm sure they do love you. In their own selfish way,' she added sotto voce.

'And Sarah is a darling, really.'

'As I said, Calypso, it is a real tribute to you that you always seek out the good in others. That is the nature of the creative soul.'

Portia had distinguished herself at the tournament in Brighton on Saturday, which meant Bell End softened his position towards me a little bit. When I say softened, he was still coming at me with two sabres and yelling things to me along the lines of, 'It's your love life or your life, Kelly! Your choice, my privilege! Hah, hah, hah!' My torso and arms now had a sort of blue mottled appearance – a look more fetching on a marble statue than a real, live girl, I suspect. I gathered from Portia that the scouts were still hot on the scent of Bell End's talent (me), and he was gearing up for the Regionals in a big way.

After our practice session on Monday, Portia and I agreed that our training had taken on a sinister military aspect we weren't entirely comfortable with. And I don't just mean physically. I suppose this wasn't helped by Bell End referring to us as Sergeant Briggs and Private Kelly.

'Why can't I be a sergeant?' I asked, because, well, Private Kelly sounded a bit pervy to me.

'You'll get your stripes when you've earned them, Private. When you've shown your general that it's sabre first, second and third for you. No boys, no life, git it?'

'Oh yes, I "git" it, Sir,' I replied petulantly.

'That's General to you, Private.'

'I suppose I always knew he was insane, but this is too much,' I said to Portia as we changed after practice.

'I love him. I think he's really determined to help us through the Regionals, you know. Seriously, it's as if it's personal for him. How's your mother, by the way?' she asked, peeling off her breeches.

'Better,' I replied. 'I mean, she's found a job which she's really excited about. Only it's not writing. She's on the *Ricky and Trudie* show doing the "What's Happening in Hollywood" slot.'

Portia grimaced. 'Be careful, darling. If Honey gets wind that your mother's on a daytime television programme, she'll torture you mercilessly. You know what a venomous snob she is about television. As far as she's concerned, it's right up there with High Street labels.'

'Or even as bad as people who don't have their own personal stylists?' I joked.

'Darling, I'm serious. She'll go for the jugular.'

After we showered, I headed off to the pet shed to give little Dorothy a run. Georgina was already there. 'Calypso, I heard about your mother. I'm really sorry.'

I looked at her dumbfounded. 'What's happened?' I asked, terrified she'd finally been carted off in a pram.

'Honey told me she's on some chavie television programme. I stood up for you, of course. As if Sarah would do something as lame as that,' she told me. 'But she's telling everyone, darling. Here, hold Dorothy. She's been telling me about how much she misses you, haven't you, bunnikins?'

I took my darling rabbit and stroked her softer-than-soft ears. She wriggled her nose and gave me a little nip. 'I think she wants a run,' I suggested. 'Have you fed her?'

'Yes, but only a bit. I hoped you'd come so you could feed her the other half. But, darling, what are we going to do about Honey and these hideous rumours?'

'The thing is,' I began as Dorothy hopped happily about the pet run, 'it's true. Sarah *is* doing the "What's Happening in Hollywood" slot on *Ricky and Trudie*.'

Georgina laughed. 'Brilliant. I love that slot. I bet

Honey's seethingly jealous that she's not on a show with "What's Happening" in the title. Let's all make a point of asking Miss Bibsmore to record it for us so we can watch it after prep. That way we can get one over on Honey and say how marvellous we think Sarah is. I bet Portia will be up for it, and Clemmie.'

'Well, Clemmie will cheer for anything,' I agreed.

'This is going to be soooo cool!' Georgina laughed.

Sure enough, as soon as we saw Honey at supper she began going on about my plebbie mother and her chavie job. 'It's poor, tragic Calypso we must rally around,' she opined to all the girls at our table, as if she really, really cared about me.

Everyone, apart from Clems, pretended to be as shocked as Honey was. Clemmie had to be led away by Arabella though, because she'd snorted her soup out her nostrils with uncontrollable laughter.

Miss Bibsmore had been only too delighted to oblige us with recording Sarah's slot. After prep, when she invited us to the television room to see Sarah's debut, Honey was caught on the back foot.

Sarah was wearing a bright red suit with enormous shoulder pads, which must have been excavated from the eighties. She'd also done something worryingly weird with her hair.

'Oh, poor Calypso,' Honey bleated. 'Sarah looks like a tragic attempt at Jackie Collins.'

'I think she looks utterly Hollywood, darling,' Georgina insisted loyally.

'Quite,' Honey agreed as if she and Georgina were of the same mind.

Actually, it turned out Sarah wasn't as embarrassing as I feared she'd be. In fact, she seemed to have her Hollywood banter down pat as she spoke easily about Brad this and Tom that and Madonna the other. 'Of course Jude is lovely in person, but well, so many Hollywood men seem to think marriage and children are just another role they're playing,' she said at one point. I couldn't help thinking that this remark was meant more for Bob than poor Jude.

'Never mind, darling,' Honey soothed, when Sarah's slot ended. 'Your mother has to do what she has to do to make ends meet. We all know of your sad upbringing, and we forgive you. I'm sure no one of our world need ever know how low Sarah has stooped this time.' Then she gave me a cuddle.

I just kept chanting away to myself: Freds loves me, Freds loves me, Freds loves me. Then later on, I added a vicious and cutting diatribe about the cruelty of 'Sweetie' in my competition essay.

This essay was proving to be truly cathartic.

TWENTY

Saint Augustine's Fencing Army Engages the Enemy

Two marvellous things happened on Saturday. Firstly, my mobile phone privileges were reinstated. Secondly, Sarah (dressed as an American cheerleader, pom-poms and all), Sister Regina (who had made a sweet little knitted flag with 'Go Calypso and Port' embroidered across it – I guess she ran out of room for the 'I' and the 'A'), Bell End, Portia (Sergeant Briggs) and myself (Private Kelly) set off to Eades in the school mini-bus for the Regionals. In other words, I was about to see Freds.

Freds, who loved me.

'So what's the deal with Freds, darling? Are we to run away or attack him this time?' asked Sarah conspiratorially.

Bell End blasted us before I could answer. 'Attack, of course. Always attack, attack, attack! None of my troops will be running away. Never heard such rot.'

'Actually, I really want you to meet him properly this

time,' I told Sarah, who clapped her hands with glee. I hoped I was making the right decision.

'Right, Private,' said Bell End, 'you and the sergeant collect your kit. I'll head in and start the reconnaissance. In the event of any questions, Private, refer to your superior officer, in this case Sergeant Briggs.'

I rolled my eyes. Not just because of the madness he was spouting but because he was wearing a red beret and had some kind of riding crop made of plastic tucked under his arm like a real general's cane.

'I'm still the captain of this team,' I reminded him.

'This is a new game plan, Private. All carefully crafted while you were running around drunk as a skunk in robes with Eades boys. I won't brook any argument when it comes to strategy, understood?' He was glaring at me so hard I backed down. 'Sister and Sarah, you come in with me to act as cover,' he barked. 'And none of that banner business this time. We'll be presenting a professional dignified front in this battle.'

'Ooooh yes, Mr Wellend,' clucked Sister Regina, hiding her knitted flag behind her back. She was obviously madly impressed by General Bell End's new persona. Nuns are soooo guileless.

Registration passed without incident, and as soon as Portia – sorry, Sergeant Briggs – and I were kitted out we looked about for our boyfriends. There were probably about a hundred fencers in the hall. Between them, the presidents armed with clipboards, the gaggles of fan clubs and not to forget, Bell End's scouts and spies lurking ominously in the shadows (well, according to Bell End anyway) we couldn't see Freds or Billy before the pools were called.

Portia and I began our stretches while the names were read out. Bell End, Sarah and Sister stood by as unobtrusively as a short man in a red beret, a nun with knitted flag and a middle-aged woman in a teen cheerleader's outfit can. Portia and I both got a really high seeding, so that by the time the direct eliminations began the wind was truly in our sails. Because this was Eades and not Sheffield, I felt I had more of a reputation at stake. Jam-smeared banners were fine in a county I was unlikely to return to, but this was my manor – well, the manor I pulled fit boys from.

I won my first direct elimination bout, effortlessly dispatching seed number sixty-five at fifteen-one. And I only allowed her that one hit because I thought she was about to cry.

Portia won hers too, and Sarah and Sister began jumping with glee.

'Good show, Sergeant Briggs, Private Kelly. But don't let your guard down. Constant vigilance, as you never know what your enemy has planned. They set traps, these scum,' he warned, looking around at the friendly faces of the girls milling about the hall. 'Oh yes, I've been eavesdropping on some of the conversations, and they're a bloody nasty lot, these girls. As nasty a lot as you'll ever see.'

That was when a girl from Saint Leonard's came skipping over to say hi to Portia. 'Darling, I just got through by the skin of my teeth. How's Tarkie, I haven't heard from him for a –'

Bell End dived over, wedging himself between the two girls. 'Sergeant Briggs, go and join Majors Sarah and Regina. I won't have my troops subverted by the likes of you,' he growled at Portia's friend.

'Don't worry about him,' I told the poor girl as I led her away. 'He goes a bit mad during these competitions.'

'Bloody nutter. You should report him. And what's with that beret and the plastic magician's stick?' she asked.

'Yes, the beret is a new touch. It, erm, goes with the pom-poms on the cheerleader, though,' I told her, pointing out my mad madre's attire.

My next bout was with a much hardier opponent. I'd fenced her before in Sheffield and she knew my form as well as I knew hers. She was slighter and shorter than me and devilishly swift to boot. I had to stretch myself to the limit for every one of the hits I made. Eventually I clenched the victory at fifteen-thirteen, but I was bruised and tired at the end.

I went over to the refreshment table for a juice. Freddie was already there, looking pretty glum until he saw me with my sweaty hair plastered to my head.

'How's it going?' I asked, trying not to be shallow and obsess on my sweaty, dishevelled appearance. I suspected it wasn't going well for Freds, despite the fact that he looked as fit as ever and his hair was still doing that lovely sticky-up thing that always made my tummy flip.

'I'm already out, rinsed by a snotty little Harrovian.'

'At least it wasn't a Wimbledonian,' I offered, which made him laugh.

'I've got a break before the semi-finals,' I told him.

'Well, then, my champion, would you like to take a short perambulation around the back of the scoreboards. I hear that's where they fix the scores.'

'And hide from the scouts and spies,' I joked. I'd told Freddie all about my mad fencing master's paranoid delusions.

'Well, then, it's a duty more than a pleasure, really, when we think of it like that. Can't let these horrid spies go unchecked.'

So we snuck around the back of the hall, avoiding Bell End and company until we reached the large blackboard. It was only used for recording the scores of school matches, as it wasn't that big, but it provided the perfect hiding spot for a pulling session.

'I forgot how lovely you smell,' Freds told me as he drew me into his stinky neck – only it smelled lovely to me. I seriously doubted my smell was lovely, though. But the fact that he said it made me swoon with love for him even more, so I blurted, 'I love you!'

Freds pulled away from me and, for a horrifying moment I thought he was going to do a runner, he looked so baffled.

But he didn't run off, he just smiled and then wrapped his arms around me so hard that he lifted me off the ground. 'So does that mean I get a formal introduction to your mother?'

'How do you know she's here?'

'Something about the pom-pom-laden cheerleader dress.' He shrugged. 'She has that Kelly look about her.'

I don't know why this pleased me so much. I guess it was

relief or something that I didn't have to hide such an important part of my life (Freds) from one of the most important people in my life. So I kissed him some more.

TWENTY-ONE

Pulling Princes

As our lips roamed over one another, I was vaguely aware of announcements being made, but I remained otherwise oblivious to everything apart from Freds. That is, right up until the point at which his lips were cruelly wrenched from mine by Bell End, who thwacked HRH with his stupid faux riding crop.

I mean, seriously, that had to be illegal for a start! Striking a royal presence?

I didn't need to seek confirmation on this. Freddie's security dived on my general and began beating him to a pulp. It was soooo unfair because Bell End didn't stand a chance. He was so small you couldn't even see him under Freddie's men. Not that a pile-up of chino-wearing thugs with earpieces were going to shut our doughty general up.

He kept yelling, 'Subversion! Foul play! Bad form! Alert the BFA!' as he valiantly flailed about with his broken plastic riding crop. Eventually the stun guns and batons defeated him, though, and nothing more than the odd squeak could be heard.

'Freds! You've got to call them off,' I begged, clutching Freddie's arm. 'That's my general!'

Freds looked at me like I was insane. 'Your what?'

'My fencing master. Bell End.'

'Oh, right. Shit! OK, chaps, that's enough,' he yelled, kicking the brutes on top.

'I'm really sorry, Calypso,' he said kissing my forehead as he kicked his thugs, 'but they have authority to act in what they consider my best interest in matters of security. It would seem they've assessed your general as a class-A threat. All we can do really is wait it out, and obviously I'll cover any, erm, medical requirements.' He gave his men a few more kicks with his foot, though.

The real salvation came in the form of Majors Sister and Sarah, who launched themselves on Fred's thugs with a professional level of violence that was really quite shocking. Within thirty seconds, Sister Regina had one of the guys in a headlock while Sarah began stuffing her pom-poms in his mouth.

By the time Sister and Sarah had called it a day, most of Fred's security guys had pom-poms up their noses and another was entwined in Sister's knitted flag. Another was nursing a bitten ear, although I think that might have been the work of Bell End.

The whole hall was gathered around our group by this stage.

Some idiot with a clipboard made a daft remark about Bell End and his friends bringing the sport into disrepute with their brawling, which only set Bell End (his beret now askew) off again.

'Freddie, this is my mother, Sarah,' I said (with a fair amount of pride, I might add) as I pushed her forward in her little mini-skirt.

Freddie took her hand, and Sarah simpered away as he kissed it. 'What a long awaited pleasure, Mrs Kelly.'

'Oh, call me Sarah, Your Royal Highness,' giggled my mad madre, giving Freds her best approximation of a curtsey while all around us fencers and their fans were dashing from piste to piste for matches and names that were being announced over the loudspeaker.

'Don't be so daft, Sarah,' Sister Regina told her gruffly, pulling her away. 'He's just like anybody else. He's not a saint, woman. Where's your Catholic pride?' Sister demanded. None of the nuns are particularly keen on boys or royalty, so Freds was not a hit with my little nun.

As I watched the two of them hitting it off, I couldn't for the life of me believe I was ever terrified of Sarah and Freds meeting. I guess knowing he loved me had made me more secure. They were flirting so ferociously I almost got jealous before I remembered that it was *me* he was pulling, not Sarah. I didn't get to witness their meeting for long, though, as my name was called and I had to weave my way through the crowds to the other end of the hall.

My opponent, her fan club lined up behind her, was already doing a few low lunges on the piste when I arrived. As we sized up for the first play, I was still distracted by recent events. Then Freddie and Sarah turned up, and Freddie cupped his hands and called out, quite loudly so everyone could hear, 'Give me a C! Give me an A! Give me an L! Give me a Y! Give me a P! Give me an S! Give me an O! Goooooo Calypso!' And a few of my opponent's fans wolf-whistled at Sarah, who was doing her cheerleader stuff beside him.

At that point things became clear. I might not have a fan club the size of my opponent, but I had something better. I had a prince who loved me.

I shook hands with my opponent, unable to hold back my happiness. I was grinning from ear to ear as I told her I hoped she'd do brilliantly. This love business had somehow taken the killer instinct out of me. My opponent wasn't brimming with the same good will towards me, though. She squeezed my hand so hard it really hurt. 'Good luck, *bitch*, you're going to need it,' she warned me sweetly. There was something about her sickly faux sweetness which reminded me of Honey.

'Thanks for the warning, daaarling,' I replied sarcastically, dragging out 'darling' with as much contempt as I could. I wasn't going to be beaten by a toxic Honey-clone in front of Freds.

Fifteen points later, she was resplendent in her humiliation. And I told her so. 'Losing becomes you, daaarling,' I whispered as we shook hands – right after she had said, 'You were lucky, that's all!'

Lucky? Me? Hello, which one of us was writing an essay on the great tragedies of her life? Me, that's who. Freddie swung me around and snog-aged. Then he held my sweaty face in his hands and said, 'Did I tell you I love you even more when you win?'

'Unhand that sergeant!' Bell End yelled. Neither of us took any notice. I was only a private, after all. It was only when he began slapping us with his beret did we realise our mistake. Making it to the finals had apparently earned me a promotion. I was now a sergeant too.

We all repaired to the refreshment table, where Portia ran up to me and said, 'Guess what! I've made it through to the finals, darling! Can you believe it?'

'OMG! Me too!'

'Aaaah!' squealed Portia with an uncharacteristic loss of her aristocratic demeanour as we kept hugging one another and jumping up and down on the spot.

'This is huge!' I said. 'We're against each other!'

'I know, let's go to the loo,' she suggested.

We didn't stop to share our news but dashed and darted through the crowds and into the loos, where we splashed ourselves with water and gave one another blow-by-blow accounts of our triumphs. It was as if we were just about to play a practice bout or something. There wasn't a bit of competitive tension between us. Maybe because we'd got all that out of our system before half-term?

'You do realise that this poses a rather nasty conundrum for our fans, though, Calypso.'

I put my hand over my mouth in horror. 'How's Bell End going to abuse us? He just made me a sergeant, you know.'

We made our way back to the refreshment table where Sister and Sarah were stuffing themselves with Battenberg cakes and tea, chatting to Freds ten to the dozen, crumbs flying everywhere.

'I watch your mother's television slot,' Freds told me.

'He thinks I'm really fit, which mean "hot",' she explained, a blush spreading across her face. 'Apparently all the boys at Eades do – think I'm fit,' Sarah boasted, giggling like the teenager she so seriously wasn't.

'Well, you are a damn fine-looking woman, Major. Don't need a bunch of wet-behind-the-ears schoolboys telling yer that, do you?' Bell End remarked. He was wearing his beret again and had his silver Olympic medal out, but his little plastic stick was now in two parts, broken by the royal thugs. Even so, he looked very impressive.

'You're a handsome little chap yourself, Mr Wellend,' Sister Regina told him sweetly.

'We've been working on our battle chants,' Sarah whispered conspiratorially to me. 'We don't want to favour either of you. I hope you don't mind, darling, but the general says that, even though I'm your mother, I'm not to show favouritism.'

'No, of course,' I agreed happily.

'You do understand,' she added. 'Portia needs our support too.'

'Fine,' I breezed, blissfully ignorant of what awaited us.

'Your fabulous legs run in the family, then,' Freds remarked sexily in my ear.

'Don't be so pervy. How dare you look at my mother's legs!' I teased.

'Well, there's not a lot else to look at, is there? I mean, to look at her, she's all legs.'

I looked over at my mother. He had a point.

When our names were called to the piste, Portia and I made our way there arm in arm. A phalanx of the fittest boys England has to offer had assembled in great numbers all around the piste, presumably with the intention of watching the final. I recognised Billy, Kev, Malcolm and a few others, but the mass was just soooo daunting.

Portia and I knew each other's form so well we could impersonate one another. As we pulled our masks down before the president had even called play, I knew that thought must be on Portia's mind too. We had the same master, we were one another's practice partners. We could match each other skill for skill. Portia's technique was flawless, and I knew that I would have to raise my thinking level beyond textbook tactics if that buzzer was to blare for me fifteen times.

There were no cheers or cries of abuse as we advanced. I emptied my mind and entered a state of pure focus in which all that existed was my blade and her blade. Portia knew only too well my preference for attack. I loved the aggression of sabre, whereas Portia had spent three years as an épéeist and loved a genius riposte. Her defence was flawless, and I knew she was relying on me to attack. So fighting aggressively against my friend in this bout would be playing to her strengths.

I had to draw her out with a bluff.

I straightened my arm to threaten her target area, but I didn't advance, goading her to attempt to clear my blade. As Portia stepped forward to beat my blade, I surprised her with a disengagement and landed a viper-quick strike to her wrist. The buzzer was the only applause required.

It was a tiring, strategic battle, fought almost as much in our minds as on the piste. It really was as Professor Sullivan, our old master, had always warned: a physical game of chess.

By the time the president called 'Fourteen, fourteen, bout point!' we were both drained physically and mentally. Everything hinged on the next three seconds, and yet behind my mask I was smiling. I was proud not just of myself but because whatever happened in the next few moments we were both going to the Nationals.

Portia's poise betrayed none of her strategic intent. But I knew that aloof demeanour now. I knew what she was about to do – or so I thought. I planned to draw her out again – after all, I was the aggressive fencer – but Portia surprised me. No sooner had the president called play than Portia leaped forward, delivering a terrifying volley of attacks, and though I parried successfully there was no way I could have landed a riposte. She was like a lunatic samurai. Bollocks to her aloof demeanour, this was war.

With a flash of insight, I trapped her blade in an envelopment, giving me that micro-second to plan my next move. Portia disengaged, readying herself for her next assault, but she'd betrayed herself, and it was too late. My blade flicked across her stomach in a deft attack she could never have anticipated. The buzzer trumpeted my victory, and the crowd erupted into tumultuous applause.

The president formalised my win. 'Fifteen-fourteen, victory Kelly.'

I tore off my mask, spraying my adoring crowd with a deluge of sweat as I saluted Portia with an old-world flourish, and then the president with the standard casual flick. Portia, her hair as disgusting as mine, ran forward and, dispensing with the formal handshake, swept me up in a cuddle. A cuddle that soon turned into a group hippie hug when Bell End, Sarah, Sister, Freddie and Billy joined us. Even Malcolm whisked me into a whirl. 'Miss Kelly, what a killer you turned out to be!'

'Thanks, Malcolm, that's really sweet.'

'So, thing is, can you give this DVD to that scrumptious friend of yours, Indie?'

'Yaah, sure,' I said, slightly dazed.

'Cool. See you round, then.' He waved as he turned to leave, and I watched his distinctive head of red hair disappear into the crowd.

It was all a whirl of congratulations, adulations and cup presentations after that. I had to stand on a stage for the ceremony as all the boys clapped for me. Freds was at the front with Portia and Billy, clapping and whistling madly. Bell End was sobbing uncontrollably with pride, although my mother and Sister Regina tried to console him. My only regret was how sweaty I was.

TWENTY-TWO

Sarah's Car of Shame

After the match, I wondered if I would ever get over such a high. Freds loved me. I loved Freds. I was going on to the Nationals and best of all, so was Portia. It was a fairy tale come true. Portia even chucked her aloof demeanour again that night back in the dorm for a celebratory party in Georgina, Star and Indie's room.

It was Tobias's idea. These things usually are.

'But I thought he'd given up drinking?' I remarked, referring to his recent bout in detox.

'He's fallen off the wagon, darlings,' Georgina explained, covering Tobias's ears. Her lower lip wobbled with the faux sorrow of it all. 'I think the best cure might be for him to let off a bit of steam, don't you?'

We most certainly did. Piling our tuck and Body Shop Specials in the middle of the room, Indie offered to do the DJ-ing, which essentially meant sticking CDs in her laptop. Soon everyone, including Portia, was dancing on the beds wildly. Honey took her usual dancing spot by the mirror so she could see herself better. Or as Star whispered in my ear, 'She's checking that she still has a reflection.'

Nothing could spoil our high that night. Even Miss Bibsmore was late doing her rounds. When she did pop her head in, all she did was tell us that while we deserved a 'bit of a party', we should try and keep the noise down.

I had to concede that Honey said nothing bitchy to me all evening. Well, nothing at first. Even when I tried on Indie's cool mini-skirt and it was too tight around the hips. She even asked if she could cadge a ride from me to Windsor the next day. Sarah was picking me up to take me to lunch with Freds. That's why I was trying on Indie's clothes, to find something truly stupendous to wear.

'I want something that says I'm stunning and wonderful and lovable,' I explained to my friends.

'And I have a wonderful house in Clapham, darling. You must come and stay, Your Royal Highness. We'll get out our best serviettes and you can sit in the lounge and watch some chav telly,' Honey added in a common accent.

I knew I'd been naïve to think she could resist taking the piss forever.

'You do such a great chav accent, darling,' Star marvelled. 'Scarily good in fact. Are you sure you don't have a little chav blood in your gene pool?'

Honey looked like she wanted to mace Star, but instead all she did was laugh as if she thought Star were really funny. Then she turned to me and said, 'So, you and the adorable Sarah are lunching with Freds tomorrow, are you?'

'We're meeting up for a pizza, if that's what you mean by "lunching",' I said.

'Poor Sarah.' Honey sighed, pausing presumably to think up what her next spiteful remark could be.

'I love Sarah,' Georgina interrupted as she danced around the room with Tobias, who was already pretty tipsy by the look of him. 'She's cool. Tobias adores her too,' she added as she did a dance spin with Tobias and fell dizzily on to the floor. 'He's a marvellous dancer, but I think he's had too much to drink,' Georgina continued, which I think was her way of changing the subject. Georgina is about the only person Honey is scared of. Georgina said that's because she knows where the bodies are buried. Star used to say that's because Georgina helped her bury them. But that was before Star decided that Georgina was cool, after all.

We finally went to bed around midnight, but Portia and I were still too high to go to sleep, so we went over and over our triumphs of that day, speculating on what the Nationals would be like and trying not to get too overexcited in case we didn't do well.

On Sunday we had a full fry-up for breakfast. Portia and I were eating loads more than we were used to, but all I seemed to do was get skinnier and taller.

After Mass finished at one, Sarah arrived in the car of shame to pick up me, Portia and Honey. Portia was lovely and gracious, of course, but Honey was sooo Honey, I could have thumped her.

Actually I could have thumped Sarah too, when I saw what she wearing.

OK, I love her. She's the best, but a powder-blue floral

skirt and matching jacket with a powder-blue handbag and pillbox hat?

'Have you been to Oxfam, Sarah?' I asked crossly.

'What are you talking about, Calypso?' Sarah replied, patting the monstrosity on top of her head. But as she looked around the faces of everyone milling around us, the gravity of her mad outfit began to sink in. 'Honey called me last night and told me that it was royal protocol to, erm, dress like the queen when meeting royals.'

Honey giggled.

Portia said nothing.

'Royal protocol?'

We were standing beside the car of shame in the car park where taxis were pulling in to pick girls up for trips into Windsor. Honey wasn't the only person laughing.

Actually the only people *not* laughing were Portia, Sarah and myself. Even the taxi drivers gathered in the forecourt were having a good chuckle.

Sarah was clearly flustered, and with everyone pointing and giggling she began to cry.

I turned on Honey. 'You are such a bitch,' I told her. 'How dare you torture my mother, you sick psycho toff.'

Honey began filing her nails. 'Don't you hate cuticles, darling? I mean, what do they even do?' she asked.

Portia spoke up before I could grapple the file off Honey and stab her with it. 'Sorry, Sarah, sorry, Calypso, but I forgot something. I'll be back in one minute. Don't leave without me,' she said before dashing back into the dorm.

'Don't worry,' I said, between clenched teeth, 'The only person we'll be leaving without is *you*,' I told Honey.

Honey rolled her eyes. 'God, I was only joking. Who would have thought anyone could be soooo stupid as to believe that you have to dress like the queen to eat pizza with the prince?'

Poor Sarah. 'Look, Mummy, you get in the car while we decide what to do. Honey, you bugger off.'

'Don't be insane, I'm coming into Windsor with you. You've offered me a lift and, if I don't go with you, I'll have no one to go with.'

'Good,' I told her as I climbed into the car and slammed the door, locking her out.

Honey was banging on the car doors when Portia returned. I let her in on the other side and she chucked a pair of jeans and a hoodie over to Sarah. 'You can wriggle into these in the car. You can pull over at Windsor Great Park – you know, where they play polo before we turn off into Windsor. I've brought some trainers too. My feet are enormous so anyone can fit into them, more or less.'

'Oh, thank you Portia, dear. You really are a super girl. I won't forget this.'

'Just drive, Mummy,' I told her.

Honey was still banging on the window of the car of shame as we drove out of the car park. It was with some satisfaction that I watched her run into a puddle as she was chasing us down the gravel drive.

Lunch was perfect. Freds found everything about Sarah

hilarious – in a good way. Even when she started explaining to him about leaving Bob, he was really sweet and sympathetic. I was ashamed that I had been embarrassed of my mother. He even asked Sarah for a signed photograph of herself to pin on his board. 'You're quite the star at Eades at the moment. Malcolm records your Hollywood slot, and we all watch it. Your interview with Tom Hanks was hilarious, especially when you kept asking him about his interest in Scientology.'

'I get my Toms confused.'

'Easily done,' Freds agreed.

After pizza, Sarah was so cool she even went off to look at the shops so that Freds and I could spend some 'quality time' together. I still couldn't believe I had been such a paranoid bitch, not wanting her to meet my boyfriend. I have the best mother in the world, even if she does drive the car of shame.

TWENTY-THREE

The Clapham Commoners

Unfortunately the car of shame wasn't big enough to squeeze in Star, Indie, Georgina, Tobias, Portia, Clemmie, Arabella, Honey, all the pets and me on our journey to London on the exeat weekend. So Sarah picked us all up in a fleet of taxis, and we rode to Clapham on the train.

Sarah chatted away happily about what she'd done to the house. 'You're going to love it, Boojie,' she enthused. 'It's right on the Common,' she added.

I was stroking Dorothy, so I missed the look on Honey's face as she giggled.

'How perfect that a commoner like you should live on the Common.'

'Yes, isn't it? Those houses are as rare as hens' teeth,' Sarah explained, missing the jibe.

Honey couldn't stop giggling, so Star draped Brian over her, which calmed her right down. 'I think he likes you,' Star said as she menaced Honey's nose with Brian. Honey's sharp intake of breath was hilarious. It wasn't often we got a treat like this.

We got off the train at Waterloo and took two black cabs to Clapham. As we wound our way into the area, I noticed a strong police presence and notices asking for information on murders and rapes. Honey opened the window and waved to the bobbies on their beat.

'Darling,' she said to me, 'what a lovely area, and imagine, you even have your own police force in bulletproof armour.'

I ignored her and pretended I was texting Freds, which I wasn't, because I'd already sent him a text he hadn't replied to yet, and I didn't want to appear tragic.

As we pulled up in front of the largest house on the Common, I was struck by how lovely it looked. Honey was delighted too as she moaned. 'Oh dear, Victorian architecture. How pokey. I can't bear modern architecture. Anything post-Georgian makes me cringe,' she groaned, visibly shivering.

'Wow,' Georgina gasped as she climbed out of the cab with Tobias. 'It's really big.'

Tobias looked impressed too.

Sarah was excited as she opened the door and ushered us all in. 'Isn't this super, our first official house party!' She giggled like a small girl.

'I'd hardly call it a house party,' Honey sneered as she cast her gaze around the lack of marble floors and wall-to-wall antiques.

'I've tried to make it comfy,' Sarah explained.

'I can tell,' replied Honey, picking up a Galle replica lamp and grimacing.

'Oh cool, a plasma television and DVD,' Indie said, rushing over and looking through the collection of DVDs. 'Sarah, is this the show you worked on in the States?'

'Yes, it was nothing wonderful, I assure you, Indie, but it paid the fees.'

Honey enveloped Sarah in a hug. 'Poverty must be so harsh, Sarah. I can tell that just by looking at the enormous pores on your skin. I can't imagine the envy that must wrack your every waking moment. Always knowing that you will never amount to anything, no matter how hard you try. Mediocrity is the death of creativity, Mummy says.'

'Oh, so that's how your soul died, is it, darling?' Star asked. 'Actually, Honey,' she added looking at her watch, 'isn't it time for your formaldehyde injection?'

Honey was, as ever, a little slow with her comeback, and Star was pulling off her Doc Marten boots and flopping on the big, squishy white sofa by the time Honey made a sneering retort.

Everyone ignored her. Indie was busy loading one of Sarah's DVDs into the player, and everyone else was snuggling up on the sofa to watch. Eventually Honey announced: 'I could murder a G & T. Do you have staff, Sarah, or will you have to prepare it for me yourself?' I almost giggled at her attempt at a sympathetic pout.

Sarah wasn't taking any more nonsense from Honey, though. 'I'll need to see your ID before I can do that, Honey. I don't support underage drinking, and while you're in my home you'll live by my rules.'

'Fine,' Honey snapped. 'You tragic Americans. I don't know how you put up with yourselves. Have you never heard of the word "hospitality"?'

Sarah ignored her.

'Oh, all right, I'll get it myself! Where's the kitchen?' she demanded, flouncing out of the room.

I made a sign to Sarah to ignore her. I couldn't bear the thought of putting up with Honey and my poor madre at loggerheads all weekend. If a drink would slow down Honey's brain, a drink she must have.

Sarah was catching on. 'Oh, I am sorry, Honey,' she called out. 'But without the staff to show me around, I haven't managed to find the kitchen yet.'

Everyone (apart from Honey) laughed at this, especially me. The weekend was getting off to a rather good start.

Later, Georgina insisted we all check out the house. 'Come on, Sarah, show us around,' she begged, pulling Sarah up off the sofa. 'Tobias is a real sticky beak, so you'll have to lock up anything you don't want him to poke about in.'

'And can we let Dorothy, Brian and Hilda wander around, Sarah?' Star enquired.

'Hilda is the, erm, rat, isn't she?' Sarah asked lightly, but I could tell she was slightly anxious.

'Well, theoretically. She's madly bright, though. You should see her on her little wheel,' Star told her as she pulled Hilda from her pocket.

I could tell Sarah wanted to scream, but instead she reached out bravely and gave Hilda a little stroke on the

head and even managed to limit herself to a little yelp when
Hilda bit her.

'See, she adores you,' Star said and, as Hilda was already
scuttling around the sofa, there wasn't much Sarah could do
or say. 'And Brian will just follow us about,' Star added. 'He's
desperately dependent and clingy, you see.'

'Clingy!' Sarah shrieked. 'Is that safe?'

Star smiled her most adorable rock chick smile – the one
that showed her tongue-piercing. 'Oh, Sarah, you are soooo
funny. Brian's the cuddliest snake you could hope to meet.'
The next minute Brian was draped around Sarah's shoulders
like a feather boa, and Sarah didn't seem to mind. Instead
she said brightly, 'Let's have that tour.'

The house turned out to be enormous. Not all the rooms
were furnished, which suited us fine as we decided to use
the biggest one as our sleepover room. Indie suggested we
just lay down duvets and pillows. Sarah was delighted at
Indie's suggestion and offered to add an Arabic theme with
rugs and bowls of Lebanese sweets.

We'd arranged to meet up with Billy, Kev, Freds and
Malcolm on the KR. Given my poverty, I suggested we take
the bus, as if that might actually be fun, cramming in with
a lot of strangers on a freezing bus in our skimpy mini-skirts
and heels.

Sarah gave us directions to the bus stop, but our lack of
street-smart savvy landed us miles away. Honey was whining,
of course, but so was Tobias, who can't bear being lost. Even
Indie lost her temper, and told off her security guys for
being incompetent. Our mood wasn't helped by the drug-

warning boxes perched on lampposts which blared out threatening messages about the dangers of finding ourselves in prison should we wish to purchase drugs.

'I'd like to purchase some drugs,' Honey declared. 'I wonder if that nice man over there in the baggy trousers and balaclava on his head could help us? As he's your neighbour, Calypso, perhaps you should ask?'

I didn't deign to reply, but I had to admit the area *was* pretty dodgy in parts. Smart, gentrified houses and chichi boutiques were cheek to jowl with council estates and crack dens and not a black cab in sight. Eventually we climbed on a bus, but we were half an hour late for the boys, who had already finished off their lattes by the time we caught up with them in one of the seventy-two Starbucks on the KR.

After the compulsory air kissing we headed off down the KR. Freddie and Indie had their security guys stay a decent distance away from us, but they seemed incapable of blending in and kept bumping into us and stumbling over one another.

After a while they began to get on Indie's nerves. 'You look like something out of *Reservoir Dogs*. Can't you at least try and blend in a bit?' Indie demanded crossly.

Even though I was getting used to being trailed by security guards, I didn't think I'd like having to live with them, especially during breaks, when a girl needed to pull a boy. And Indie was definitely determined to pull Malcolm.

Between all of us we knew every second person we passed. My lips got quite numb with all the *mwah-mwah-mwah*-ing we did. We went into the Cadogan Arms so that

Honey could satisfy her craving for a drink, and then we went to Partridges to find some more trendy outfits that we could share.

The boys were coming back to Clapham with us, and Freds had the bright idea that it might be fun to try public transport. Malcolm came up with the bright idea of disguising themselves and their security guys with lipstick and eye shadow. I suppose it *was* quite funny. Also it reminded me of the day Malcolm, Kev and Freds had scaled the scaffolding of our dorm house and disguised themselves as girls to fool Miss Bibsmore.

I don't know whose bright idea it was to get off at the wrong stop, but suddenly we were on Landor Road. Problem was, we'd left the security guys on the bus!

'We should wait for them, I guess,' Freds groaned, kicking listlessly at a used syringe on the street.

'They're big boys. They can take care of themselves. Besides, they've been really irritating me today,' Indie insisted, looking at Malcolm as she spoke.

Malcolm was looking at her as he had been all day. 'We'll take care of you,' he said, putting a protective arm around her. Only clearly he meant *he* planned to take care of her. She fluttered her eyelashes at him.

Freds noticed the chemistry between them too and gave my hand a squeeze. We wandered off in the direction in which the bus had vanished. At the corner, under a lamp that had had its light smashed out, we were offered drugs by a large guy with gold teeth and a hoodie pulled up over his head, Gandalf-style.

The drug-warning box we walked past was still operational and cheerfully chiming, 'You can be imprisoned for both possession and intent to supply illegal substances. Please report any drug activity to the police.'

'Skunk weed, crack?' offered Gandalf.

Malcolm turned around pleasantly and asked, 'What is skunk weed exactly?' Gandalf looked him up and down as if Malcolm were a bone he might want to chew. I began to feel scared. 'Only is it weed or is it a specific type of weed?' he probed.

'Are you shitting me, bro?' Gandalf asked, coming towards our little group with menace. He stuck his face right up against Malcolm's. 'Because I is warning you now, sunshine. I don't like to be shit.'

'No, well, I imagine you wouldn't,' agreed Malcolm in a friendly enough way. 'But I assure you that shitting you was never my intention,' he added, all easy charm. He was clearly oblivious to any sense of danger.

Freds and Billy tried to pull Malcolm away.

Star, Georgina and the rest of us – apart from Honey – lurked in the background nervously. Well, I was nervous. Star looked quite relaxed with Brian slung around her neck like a feather boa. I suppose this was all perfectly normal for the daughter of Tiger from Dirge. In fact I think one of his big hits was titled 'Scoring Skunk'.

'Come on, man,' Billy urged, tugging on the hood of Malcolm's Ralphie.

'Poncy little shit,' snarled Gandalf, grabbing the front of Malcolm's Ralphie. That was when I realised that there were a few other Gandalf clones lurking around other lampposts nearby. Then Gandalf pulled his other hand out of his pocket and I saw the gold of the knuckle duster glint as he pulled his fist back to smash Malcolm's face.

I was about to scream when Honey suddenly came forward and maced Gandalf – scoring a direct hit. But all the mace did for Gandalf was what the Febreze had done for me. It teared him up a bit but didn't completely incapacitate him. He was still holding Malcolm and now calling loudly for his brethren. So Honey maced him again, only this time she was inches away and taking a bit of a risk if you ask me. But she was as relaxed as could be as she emptied the contents of the mace can into Gandalf's face.

Howling in pain, the guy eventually let go of Malcolm and we all legged it down the road – the brethren and their injured brother in hot pursuit. For such big guys they could run pretty fast, too. One of them collared Kev and was about to launch his fist in his face when Honey smashed one of her Jimmy Choos on his head over and over again. Another of them got hold of Malcolm, but Indie jumped on his back, giving Malcolm the chance to smash his forehead into the guy's nose.

The security men eventually arrived in time to use their stun guns on the dozens of Gandalf brethren flooding out of a nearby council estate armed to the teeth with knives and God knows what else. 'Get out of here, will you!' one of the security guys yelled at us.

So we legged it, closely followed by a number of Gandalfs, but all those cross-country runs we'd been tortured with over years were starting to make sense now. I guess drugs had depleted the Gandalfs' level of physical fitness because they were slobs compared to the girls of Saint Augustine's and the boys of Eades over a longer distance. Even the security guards had more breath in them than the Gandalfs – one of whom even resorted to using a Ventolin spray, he was wheezing so badly.

We finally lost them after another hundred metres. The security guys were not impressed with us, but they were sensible enough to take us into a café and get some sweet tea into us.

We all piled into the loo at the café to clean ourselves up and fix our hair. As we were coming out we bumped into the boys, who'd all been preening themselves as well. Poor Malcolm had a torn shirt. 'Don't worry about it. I've got dozens,' he replied when Indie began to fuss.

'There is no way we can let Sarah know about what just happened, guys, OK?' I insisted.

'Why not?' Honey asked. 'She does live here. They may well be her friends,' Honey suggested.

And just when I was starting to like her for saving us from Gandalf.

'Don't be more of an idiot than you already are, Honey,' Freddie told her firmly, and she relented sulkily, even going so far as to admit she was only joking.

When we got back, Sarah threw open the door to us and sang, 'Hel-lo! I was just about to call out a search party.' She joked in blissful ignorance. 'How was your day?'

We all answered, 'Super!'

Malcolm elaborated with fanciful tales of ambassadors and caviar, which made Indie giggle. But I could tell by the looks passing between the security guys that they wanted to throttle Malcolm and Honey and quite possibly the rest of us.

As I sat there watching Honey going along with our ruse to keep the fight from Sarah, I was impressed. Could this be a new side of Honey?

'So you caught up with lots of friends, then?' Sarah enquired directly of Honey.

'Oh yes, Sarah,' Honey agreed gleefully. 'And some of your neighbours,' she added.

Everyone glared at her, imagining she was about to blow our cover.

'Air kisses all round,' Honey simpered. 'In fact, Glaswegian kisses for some, wasn't it, Malcolm?' she added just to make us squirm, I think.

'Oh, Malcolm, what are you like?' Sarah teased, completely oblivious to the undertones of the conversation and probably ignorant of what a Glaswegian kiss even was.

'Been to Glasgow, then, have you, Honey?' Malcolm asked – obviously joking.

'Darling? *Moi* go north of the M25?' Then she did that horrible laugh she does where her collagen lips bubble up. And like everyone, I breathed a sigh of relief. Honey had definitely saved our butts on the street and she was even playing along to protect Sarah from the truth. Yet deep down she was still the Honey we knew and tolerated and, funnily enough, I took an odd sort of comfort in that.

I could tell Star was thinking the same thing because she winked, first at me and then at Georgina, Portia and even Tobias while Sarah explained the games she'd set up all over the floor: Twister, Cluedo, Hungry Hungry Hippos – a whole variety of babyish games. Bless, I thought, determined not to be embarrassed.

'I thought we might all play some games?' she suggested excitedly.

'Cool,' agreed Malcolm. 'I love Hungry Hungry Hippos.'

And it *was* cool. I don't think I've ever laughed so hard as when Freds' and Indie's security guys fell into a tangled Twister heap.

The only downside of the whole weekend was that I didn't get to kiss Freds – well, not nearly enough.

TWENTY-FOUR

Bob's Big Bombshell

fter such a wonderful weekend with Sarah, I felt the need to write to Bob. Sarah had gone from a reverting infant to a brilliantly independent woman (with a bit of help from Bunny, whom I heard her speaking to on the phone). Despite all her reverting and madness, I was really proud of my mother for managing to set up a house, land a job in a country where she had no professional history, get fired and land another job which had transformed her into a minor celebrity. And all the way through she'd been there for me, taking me to lunch, supporting my fencing and impressing my friends and boyfriend.

And where was Bob during this transformation? Swanning around like an eighteenth-century dandy, draped over his wretched script, all thoughts of family responsibility forgotten. Even Freds hinted that he thought Bob was a loser.

And I couldn't have that.

Either Bob was going to have to sort himself out, or I was going to give Sarah my full support. Which meant giving Bob the boot. I think writing my essay had helped to stimulate my sense of injustice. Every night at prep after I'd done my coursework, I tackled the edits Ms Topler had suggested for my essay. I think it was when I was writing about Bob humiliating me at the navel-piercing shop in Beverly Hills that I realised I had to confront him properly. Face-to-face, even. The arrogance of the man knew no bounds, and he needed to be brought down a peg or two.

Dear Father,

Enough is enough. The only good thing you had going for you (Sarah) has set up a lovely home in a rapidly gentrifying area of London and is presenting a really cool show and is admired by teenage boys everywhere as the hottest woman on television. I plan to advise Sarah to divorce you because you suck and Sarah rocks. Put that in your script!

Yours sincerely,

Calypso

PS: Not that you'd care, but I won the Regionals and this Saturday I intend to win the Nationals at the Crystal Palace Sports Centre, which happens to be where the British Olympic team trains and Sarah will be there supporting me. She has been cheering me on at every match since she moved over here while you've been self-absorbed and unfeeling.

I studied my expertly crafted e-mail for some time, making a few minor adjustments. Bob had an eagle eye when it came to lapses in grammar. He could bang on for hours about the imperfect past participle as used in England. He should have married Ms Topler – she would have given him a run for his money. When I was sure it was just right, I pressed 'Send', revelling in the note of defiance as the mouse clicked.

I was about to go back to my essay about the great tragedy that was my life when I got a response from Bob.

Congratulations darling,

['Darling' indeed. If he thought he could sweeten me up with darlings he had a huh and a half coming his way!]

I am thrilled that both you and Sarah are flourishing in England. I am so thrilled in fact that I have just decided to come to the tournament on Saturday to see my little girl trounce the competition.

Your loving father,

XXX Bob

Oh bugger. How dare he abuse my stern, reprimanding e-mail, which was meant to make him *très* remorseful and depressed, and use it as an excuse to inflict himself on poor Sarah and stress her out just as she was starting to enjoy herself again. Bob's presence at the Nationals could be catastrophic. Stupid, stupid Calypso, for even mentioning the tournament, I scolded myself. If Bob did carry out his threat and come to the tournament and distress Sarah, it would be all my fault. I had to do something! I had to stop this.

But first I had to write a lot of really mean things about him in my essay. My fingers moved like a righteous gale over the keyboard as I poured my feelings into the essay. When it was finished, I was quite proud. Any guilt I may once have harboured over exposing my family as dysfunctional had dissolved. Just like my enthusiasm for the Nationals, I realised. After all, how could I face the Nationals with Bob there upsetting Sarah?

If Bob turned up, I was going to have to keep him away from Sarah at all costs. I decided to enlist the General to fight the good fight. Bell End was a man who didn't flinch in battle and, more importantly, he loved a paranoid delusion like no one else.

That night, while Honey was visiting her horrid sister, Poppy, I shared my fear with Portia about Bob coming to the Nationals.

Portia was more circumspect than I was about the Bob thing. 'If he's so broke, how can he afford to fly out here? And where would he stay? I doubt Sarah is going to take him back. She strikes me as being an extremely determined woman.'

'But how can I risk it? I can't focus on my fencing knowing my father and mother are involved in their own field of combat across the arena somewhere. And Sister Regina is too tiny to help.'

'Darling, you're being silly. Don't you recall what Sister did to Fred's security guards? One of them was still wearing a plaster on his nose last weekend.'

I giggled at the memory. 'This isn't funny,' I told her, snapping out of it.

She giggled too. 'It is, really.'

'I'm thinking of telling Bell End tomorrow.'

'I don't think that's a good idea,' she advised as Honey returned to our room.

I knew I was right to tell Bell End, though.

'It's the bloody BFA!' he hissed. 'They've put him up to it, I'll be damned. They've been trying to bring me down since I won this silver,' he snarled, brandishing his medal at me.

'No, actually I don't think you understand what I'm trying to explain, sir. I mean General. Bob, that's my father, and Major Sarah, well, we can't let them meet at the Nationals! It will traumatise not just Sarah but, well, every-one actually.' *Me especially*, I wanted to say.

'Bloody fine little woman, your mother. No, you leave it to me, Kelly. This goes deeper than some petty marital dispute. I've seen this sort of thing before, girl. Subversion on an impressive scale. You're still a neophyte to the ways of the BFA.'

'A what?'

'A kindergartener.'

Portia was right. I shouldn't have told him about Bob. He was insane.

He patted me on my head – no mean feat, as I towered a good six inches above him. 'You let me look after little Sarah. I'll keep this bastard Bob at bay.'

Portia came into the salle then, so our conversation was cut short, but I don't think prolonging it would have made me feel more confident.

'Right, get changed and we'll begin the drill. I can feel the spirit of Jerzy Pawlowski in the salle today, girlies.'

As we dashed towards the changing rooms, Portia joked, 'How many ways of moving forward do you have?'

But I couldn't even pretend to joke that day. The usual good humour a girl feels during the last week of Christmas term was noticeably absent for me. Not even the ebullient mood of Ms Topler as I handed in my completed essay on the last day of term had lightened my mood.

Apart from the overseas students, all the other girls had already left for the Christmas break – Portia and I had been given special permission to stay over Friday night due to the Nationals. The school felt eerily empty by Friday evening as Portia and I helped Bell End load the mini-bus, so we all jumped when Ms Topler came running outside.

'Dear child, dear, dear Miss Kelly! I wept.'

'Oh, I'm sorry,' I told her, wondering what I'd done to upset her.

'No no no, I wept tears of sorrow!' She insisted, as if this were a good thing. 'I wept tears of helplessness. I wept tears of horror.'

I knew she was referring to the essay now, but horror? Maybe I had over-egged the pudding of my tragic life a little too much.

'Yes, and finally I wept tears of pride at the tribute to literature that you placed in my hands this morning,' Ms Topler exclaimed.

'Stand away from the bus!' Bell End yelled as he manoeuvred our fencing kits in. Then he muttered something about saboteurs being everywhere. 'Only authorised fencers, Ms Topler.'

'Oh, I see. Well I'll bid you good night, then,' she replied awkwardly. 'But thank you, Calypso. I just wanted to praise your work and to assure you that I know brilliance when I read it, and what's more, I know you're going to win this competition.'

'Of course she's going to win. Haven't bin training her up to lose, yer silly woman!' Bell End yelled at my poor English literature teacher.

'Thank you, Ms Topler,' I called out as she ran towards the safety of the school.

TWENTY-FIVE

Bob at Bay

S ister Regina sat up front with Bell End on the drive to Crystal Palace sports centre in London. Sarah was going to meet us there, as it wasn't that far, coming from Clapham. I wished now that I hadn't been so specific about where the Nationals were being held when I e-mailed Bob.

As we drove past the long rows of suburban houses under Heathrow's busy flight path, I wondered if Bob had already flown in. Maybe he was already here, lurking in London somewhere?

'So, have you got a photograph of this father of yours, Kelly?' asked Bell End.

'Yes,' I admitted, passing a snap taken last summer, when all had been rosy and cosy at *chez* Kelly.

'Are you certain you want to light the fuse on this?' Portia asked me quietly as Bell End grabbed my photograph and stuck it on the rearview mirror.

'See this man here, Sister?' He jabbed at my father's smiling face.

Sister perched her pince-nez on her nose and peered at

the friendly face of Bob. He was wearing shorts and T-shirt at the beach, his arm around Sarah and me.

Sister Regina studied the photograph for some time before exclaiming. 'Oh, that's our lovely Sarah. Doesn't she look tanned? And soooo slim too. What a wonderful figure she has for a woman her age, don't you think, Mr Bell End?' Poor Sister was starting to pick up on our nickname for our master.

'I'm not interested in the blasted woman's legs, Sister,' he snapped gruffly. 'It's the man beside her.' He jabbed at my father's face again. 'Kelly's father. He intends to disrupt the finals, Sister. Sabotage us. Ruin everything. We've got to stop this man.'

Sister turned around. Her elderly face creased with years of fervent prayer and kindness.

'Is this true, Calypso? Does your father wish us ill?'

'Well, you know how my mother's left him?'

Sister nodded. 'A very sad business, although talking to Sarah I feel a great sense of love for your father inside her. And regardless of Sarah's sadness over Bob's Big One, why would your own father want you to do badly, dear?'

I blushed, worried now that I'd started Bell End off – and he was not a man to be held back. 'That's not really the point, Sister. It's just that I know it will upset Sarah seeing him at this stage, and oh, I don't know. She's had such a tough time settling back in England, Sister. And now she's finally on her feet, I don't want him bullying her.'

Sister peered more closely at the photograph. 'But he looks like such a kind man, Calypso.'

'Kind, my foot,' said Bell End gruffly. 'Man's out to sabotage us, Sister. You have to leave sentiment out of the bloody thing. Do you want our girl to fail? Do you want Major Sarah upset?'

'Oh! No, General. Dear Calypso, no. We can't have that,' Sister agreed. 'I was just saying he looks like such a nice man. But of course if he intends to muck our Sarah about or interfere with Calypso's sporting achievements, he'll meet with fierce resistance from me, General.'

'I wouldn't be surprised to learn he's been despatched by one of the competitors in a dirty-tricks campaign,' Bell End muttered.

'Isn't that a bit elaborate, Mr Wellend?' Portia asked reasonably.

'You don't know what elaborate means, Briggs. They'll stoop to anything. This is the Nationals. If you girls get through, you'll be invited to try out for the National Team. We're talking big money, not just prestige. There will be sponsorship deals; Adidas, Leon Paul, everyone will be after you. The world will be your oyster. There's a lot of money and status involved here. And people are more than happy to get their hands dirty for the sake of that as I know only too well.'

'Yes, but Mr Wellend, we're talking about Calypso's father, Bob,' Portia reminded him reasonably. 'Not a BFA saboteur!' Under her breath, she added, 'If they even exist.'

'Look,' I said, trying to steer things round to the real issue. 'I just don't want Sarah upset today, OK? Despite her own problems, she's backed me all the way this term. She's really excited about today, and I don't want Bob upsetting her.'

'Good woman is Sarah, solid gold. All right, Kelly, leave it to Sister and me. We won't let this Bob geezer get a look in, will we, Sister?'

'No, Mr Wellend. We don't want our dear Sarah upset. I'm knitting her a lovely little mauve collar.' With that she held up her knitting, and sure enough the beginnings of something mauve and ghastly were already emerging. Knowing Sarah, she'd wear it too. Bless.

'So, you just focus on your form, Kelly. Leave the externals to us. Now, how many ways of moving forward have you got, girls?'

Portia and I replied, 'As many as we need,' and were rewarded with a rare laugh from our fencing master.

Freds had sent me a text that morning wishing me luck, but I hadn't expected to see him at the event. But there he was, waiting patiently for us, along with Billy and Malcolm under the arch. I could make out his gorgeousness as we made our way on the long walk down towards the arch of the sports centre.

Despite its name, Crystal Palace isn't really a palace, nor is it made of crystal. But it is a massive complex and Freds looked dwarfed as he leaned against the arch with his friends. As he was about to give me a hug, Bell End dropped our kit and grabbed Freds by the collar of his Ralphie. 'I've got other business today, Sonny, but I've got your face etched in my mind, filed under "enemy", so don't think I'm off my guard.'

'Right, sir, I'll keep that in mind,' Freddie replied, calmly rearranging his collar.

Malcolm, who had been smoking a cigarette, flicked it on the ground and put it out with his foot. He extended his hand to Bell End. 'McHamish,' he said warmly.

'Just watch your step, mister. I've got your number so I don't need your name, git it?'

Billy didn't say anything.

Sister gave Malcolm a shy little wave. 'Aren't you a good-looking bunch of chaps? Would you like a biscuit?' She produced a tin of biscuits from under her voluminous habit. 'Sister Michael made them, so I don't recommend you try too many. The last batch she made tasted like worms. She always overdoes the coconut. Hangover from the war.'

The boys turned down her offer politely and smiled at Portia and me. Then our uneasy little party wandered through to reception, where the noise of the crowds milling round and running about was deafening. The arched ceilings made everything echo ominously. I felt like a tiny ant as I joined the queue with Portia to have our names ticked off.

After registration, I took Freds aside for a word about Bob. He was really sweet and assured me not to worry. Billy was still going through registration, so Freds called Malcolm over and the mug shot of my father was passed around once more. I suddenly felt like I was presenting my father as some kind of target to a group of hit men.

'Don't worry yourself, young Calypso, my little

champagne-quaffing chum,' Malcolm assured me. 'He won't know what's hit him if he comes within a hundred yards of you. You saw what I did to that Gandalf chap. I'll give him a Glaswegian kiss if he starts mucking the glorious Sarah about while I'm around.'

'He's not dangerous,' I shrieked. 'He's my father. I don't want him hurt or anything!' I was beginning to feel that I had ignited a fire that could never be extinguished. This is what I always do. It's what I've done all my life. 'I just don't want him upsetting Sarah,' I tried to explain as the boys were jostled away by a fencing team coming through.

Freds and Malcolm told me they were off to see if they could find Billy before saying their laters and leaving me alone. Well, not alone. I had my posse, but I still felt like a little ant in a giant hive. I didn't know my way around.

Having only come an hour away from school, Portia and I were already in our kit, but after registration we went to the loo to confab. That was where we found Sarah applying make-up – odd in itself, as she was a great believer in 'natural beauty'.

'Hello, darlings, isn't this super? You must be excited. I know I'm exhilarated by all this bustle.'

'You won't be for long,' I almost blurted. And then it turned out I'd actually said it. Typical. Stupid, stupid, stupid Calypso.

'Whatever do you mean, Calypso? Is something wrong?'

'Just nerves,' Portia assured her, giving me a warning look.

'Yes, well the adrenaline is bound to be coursing through

you, Boojie, but you have to learn to centre yourself. Find your chi.'

'My chi? And where on earth might I find my chi?' I asked, my nerves jangling around my body.

Sarah looked lost. 'Erm, well, you can find your chi any-where. It can just sneak up on you, really. The point is, nothing exists beyond the now. Remember what Bob always says?'

'Oh, I remember what Bob always says,' Portia said brightly. 'Swell.'

Sarah laughed. 'Oh dear, I do miss the old boy. I'm really quite giddy at the thought that he might turn up today to support you.'

'No, you're not,' I told my mother. 'He oppresses you!' And then I wondered how she'd got wind of his threat to turn up.

Sarah wrapped her arms around me and rocked me gently. 'Oh, Boojie, you rock my world.'

'My world is rocking, that's for sure,' I told her. 'But that doesn't answer my question.'

'Well, enough navel gazing,' Sarah insisted briskly as she grabbed Portia and me by the hands and led us out into the swarming humanity of the hall.

TWENTY-SIX

And Just as They Were Bringing in My Crown!

Portia and I passed Billy and the others en route to our pools, which were to be held in the basketball courts. It was so packed in the hall now with fencers, BFA representatives, parents, fans and Bell End's saboteurs, that no one even noticed Billy and Freds giving Portia and me a pre-match snog-age session.

Sarah spotted Sister at the cafeteria on the first floor and said she'd watch us from up there, where there was a glass front and comfy seats. Also, the scoreboards were in there, she explained. 'I saw it on the map.'

Bell End was nowhere to be seen.

I felt a tug on my arm as I was walking on the walkway towards the basketball courts. A Year Seven girl from Saint Leonard's offered me her fencing kit bag and a pen. 'Could you sign my bag please, Miss Kelly?' she asked sweetly.

'Erm, why?' I asked, confused.

'I saw your picture in *The Sword* when you won the South East Cup.'

'Oh, sure,' I agreed, signing my name, feeling like a total fraud.

After the girl left, Portia took the piss. 'When I grow up, I want to be just like you, Miss Kelly.'

I was about to laugh when I spotted him, my father, Bob, standing down in the pit, an arena where the Boys' pools were taking place. He was on his own, but Freds and Malcolm were only yards away from him. I felt this terrible, almost painful, pang of affection for my poor father in that moment. He looked so small and lost down in the pit and I was hit with memories of all the times he'd been there for me, cheering me on, applauding all my efforts. However hopeless I was at something, Bob always said, 'You did swell, Princess, just swell.' I remembered how Bob had built the little stage in the living room so I could act and do my tragic little song-and-dance routines. My rendition of 'How Much Is That Doggy in the Window?' used to have him in tears.

'Oh shit,' I said to Portia, pointing. 'There he is.'

'Bell End?'

'No, Bob. Look down in the arena.'

Portia took me by the shoulders. 'Honestly, Calypso, now is not the time to obsess about him. Sarah is fine. She's with Sister upstairs in the cafeteria.'

'But she'll see him.'

'I don't get the impression she minds. She sounded like she was looking forward to seeing him.'

I was confused but just then I could hear my name being called, so I charged off to my designated piste.

The next time I saw Bob was in the arena during my

second direct elimination bout. The boys' matches were going on down one end and the girls' were at the other. Sister and Sarah were still upstairs with their tea. Their enthusiasm for fencing must have dwindled somewhat from those heady days in Sheffield because now they were content to watch us from afar, waving vaguely as they chatted and dunked their biscuits in their tea. After all their mad enthusiasm, a part of me now felt neglected.

But I had other things on my mind. Bob knew where I was now because the announcers had insensitively called my bout over the intercom.

Bell End was furious. 'I asked them to use your code name too.'

'I don't have a code name, sir,' I reminded him.

'You do now, girl. I told them your name was Princess Jelly Bean.'

'Princess Jelly Bean? What? Couldn't you do better than that?'

'Well, I didn't want to get you mixed up with any other princesses that might be here. Figured Jelly Bean was safe.'

'It's also insane.'

'Still, the point is, that they didn't use it. Saboteurs, *see*! I warned you. I'm going up there now to sort this out. They've put you in jeopardy. This Bob will sniff you out now, no trouble.'

That reminded me. I sniffed my pits – just at the point that Freds came over with Malcolm to wish me luck.

'How's Billy doing?' I asked, wind-milling my arm as if I were merely exercising rather than pit-sniffing.

'He's still in. The last bout was close, though.'

'Got a cigarette, Calypso?' Malcolm asked.

'Are you mad?' I asked him. I was, after all, wearing a skintight white fencing outfit electrically wired and sans pockets. Quite apart from the fact that I wasn't a smoker, the only thing I could keep on my person was sweat.

'No? Oh well, Portia? Got any fags?'

Portia continued with her low lunges, not even deigning to answer his absurd request with a look.

'Bit whiffy in here,' Malcolm remarked, and then wandered off.

After trouncing my next opponent, I went up to the cafeteria with Portia, as we both had a break. Bob hadn't approached me so far, but I could feel him watching me, so I took a circuitous route with Portia up the stairs. Sister and Sarah had clearly OD-ed on tea and biscuits and were bouncing about the cafeteria like ping-pong balls.

Sarah was wearing the mauve collar that Sister must have finished. 'Look, look what Sister made me!' Sarah squealed, dancing about with glee.

The collar was too tragic for words, but I wasn't going to be the one to pop her bubble. The poor old madre may as well squeeze in what fun she could before Bob turned up to break her heart.

'It's very, erm, fetching,' I told her, trying to get her to sit and calm down.

'Oh, darling, I'm glad you like it. Today is such an exciting day, isn't it?' she asked with an intensity I put down to the caffeine.

'Yes, Sarah, it is an exciting day.'

'I have a special surprise for you too, later,' she said, bopping about like a wind-up toy.

Oh dear, I thought, fearing she'd commissioned Sister to knit me a collar too. 'Fabulous,' I said with as much enthusiasm as I could muster. 'I'm really looking forward to it.'

Portia came back with juices, and we sat down and stretched our aching muscles before our names were called again.

Bell End must have worked his magic because when the final bout was called, my name was announced as Princess Jelly Bean.

As I forced my way through the crowd on to the piste, I was aware of Sarah, Sister, Bell End, Malcolm and Freds all together. I shrugged off my concern that Bob may have already seen them, because while people weren't exactly jeering me, there was the odd bit of tittering and a few snide cries of, 'Go, Princess Jelly Bean!'

Portia had been knocked out in the semi-finals so she was there to wire me up and give me a few words of encouragement. 'Darling, don't think of anything else. This bout is all that matters to you now. Everything else can wait.'

My opponent was my old foe from the finals in Sheffield, Jenny. I feared for poor Jenny and her fans, with Bell End being as wound up as he was, but I smiled at her kindly, figuring she probably still hadn't recovered from his horrible abuse at our last match.

But I was wrong. Oh, so wrong. When we tapped one

another's equipment to make sure the electrics were working, she 'tapped' my blade clean out of my hand.

I watched as it bounced across the floor beyond the piste. OK. We were playing nasty.

'Slay the foul little bitch,' came Bell End's echoing roar, audible to everyone in the enormous arena. Sister Regina added, 'Yes, you go on and slay her, Calypso! Nasty girl, nasty girl.'

Jenny punched the air with her fist. 'You're dead meat, Jelly Bean!' she yelled to the mighty cheer of her fans.

What did she think this was, *Gladiator II*?

I put my hand out to shake hers. She twisted it behind my back and was about to threaten me, but the president stepped in and handed her a red card, meaning she had already lost herself a valuable point.

Her emotional decrepitude could only work to my advantage, I decided. Even so, there was every chance that the two of us would be asked to join the National Team regardless of who won. Actually, that would make her my fencing buddy – but I could deal with that. After all, my roommate this term had been Honey, and I'd survived her.

Just the same, my first advance was poor. The spirit of Jerzy Pawlowski seemed to have abandoned me just when I needed him most. For all Portia's encouragement, my mind wasn't focused on the game. It was on Bob and Sarah, so I couldn't believe it when I began to strip points from Jenny. Jenny's blade was a secondary consideration as I took my eyes off Jenny to search the crowd for my father. I just couldn't force myself to concentrate the way I knew I should. My brain kept telling me 'Focus!' but my heart kept telling me 'Your family needs you'.

I heard Freds yell my name, and as I turned to look, I inadvertently clipped my blade on Jenny's glove, earning me yet another undeserved point. Just as the fight was meeting its climax of thirteen, nine in my favour, I spotted Bob making his way towards Sarah.

In my horror, I stumbled backwards, clearing myself of Jenny's attack and my guard connected with the pit of her stomach. Another point to me. Fourteen-nine. It was ridiculous. I was playing like a random bluffer in a poker game, and yet it was my lack of strategy which seemed to be throwing Jenny off. Then I realised what was really happening. Jenny thought she was in combat with the girl she'd fought in Sheffield and was trying to outwit me by referring to my previous form. But the Calypso Kelly she'd fought in Sheffield was not the Princess Jelly Bean she was up against now.

And then it happened – Bob tapped Sarah on the arm, she spun around, he took hold of her shoulders and kissed her.

The president called play again, but I couldn't drag my eyes away from Bell End, who wasted no time in launching his body into Bob's, rugby tackling him to the ground. At that moment, Jenny launched into a lethal lunge. I flailed about with my blade impotently, causing her blade to run harmlessly up my left sleeve where no point could be registered. Even in my emotional turmoil, I was aware that all that stood between me and winning was one lousy point! The president was about to call halt for the sake of my arm's safety, but I brought my blade down on Jenny's shoulder before he had the chance. The victory was mine.

I tore off my mask as the buzzer blared and the crowd roared its support. Jenny threw her blade across the piste in a fit of fury as I went to shake her hand.

OK. Fine.

So to Bell End and Bob I flew. The scene that awaited me was not dignified. Bell End was rolling about the floor on top of Bob with Sarah on top of him, begging him to 'leave my man alone'.

Sister was getting in the odd kick at Bob's head, but mostly she was running around the heap, entangling their bodies with her yarn.

Neither my parents nor Sister Regina were the best of fighters, and Bell End was more of a mouthpiece for violence than a physical threat, so no *real* damage was being done. Still, it wasn't quite the dignified end to my winning the Nationals that I had envisioned.

Freds and Portia helped me pull them all apart.

'Miss Kelly,' a be-suited man said as he extended a hand to me. 'My name is Jim Baird, I represent the British National Fencing Team and I wondered –'

'Is this the blighter?' yelled Malcolm, suddenly appearing on the scene, fag in mouth.

The BFA rep took a step back, but Malcolm was pointing at Bob, who was now being dusted down lovingly by Sarah. What on earth was she thinking? If I didn't know better, I'd say she was thrilled to see him. Freds was occupied keeping Bell End in a headlock. Sister was happily rewinding her yarn into a neat ball.

'Yes, that's the subversive bastard, git him!' Bell End yelled to Malcolm, who happily obliged by removing his fag and head-butting my poor father with an effortlessness only a true Scot can carry off.

I was still holding the BFA representative's hand. 'Hello, I'm Calypso Kelly. These people have nothing to do with me.'

'No, I would hope not. Could we go somewhere quiet to speak?' he suggested.

So I went off with Jim, the BFA representative, and he asked me if I'd join the National Team. It should have been the happiest news of my life, but I couldn't shake off the image of Bob kissing Sarah, which diluted my joy considerably.

Of course I said how excited I was to be invited on to the National Team but, after we'd gone over the formalities and I'd given him my details, I immediately rushed back to the aid of my parents. I had half an hour at most to sort their marital problems out before I would have to go on the stage to collect my cup.

Sarah grabbed me in cuddle. 'Oh, Boojems, we're soooo proud of our baby, aren't we, darling?'

Darling?

'Bob has sold his Big One for two million – that's sterling, not dollars – isn't that marvellous, Calypso?' Sarah cooed like a dove. 'We reconciled last night. It was heaven.'

Sister Regina agreed it was a lot of money but I silenced her with a glare.

Two million pounds was a lot of money (well, to me it was – even if it would seemed chump change to girls like Star and my other friends), but that wasn't the point. There were principles at stake and I was nothing if not a girl jam-packed with principles.

'You don't just reconcile with someone because they sell a script for a lot of money, Sarah,' I lectured. 'And you well know it! After everything that's happened, I think you might have consulted me or at least Bunny. I'm sure she won't be too thrilled to learn that you are back with your oppressor merely because he's come into some loot,' I scolded.

'Nice to see you too, Princess Jelly Bean,' my father said.

Naturally I ignored him and turned to my boyfriend for back-up. 'Don't you agree, Freddie?'

'Sorry, what was that, Calypso?' he asked, his eyes darting about the room as he took a step backwards. 'I might just go and see what Billy's up to. Coming McHamish?' he asked, pulling on his friend's shirt.

'No, let's stay. This is interesting. Might come in handy with my ethics paper. Go on, Bob, go on, Sarah and Calypso,' urged Malcolm eagerly.

'Yes,' agreed Bell End, who looked like he wanted another go at Bob. 'Go on, *Bob.*' He spat my father's name out as if it were a gob of mucus.

All Sarah and Bob did was laugh. Yes, laugh. And what was more sickening is that they looked into one another's eyes as they laughed. After all I'd been through, trying to support Sarah, make my father see sense and deal personally with their breakup, their laughter felt like a betrayal.

'I don't see what's so funny,' I told them imperiously, standing upright in my sweaty white fencing outfit, my mask under one arm, leaning on my sabre to add a bit of authority, if not menace, to my speech.

'Oh, darling, we're not laughing at you, it's just the situation. We're happy. Truly happy. And it's not the money. Well, we're very pleased with that aspect, obviously.' Sarah giggled like a teenager.

'I really think you should consult with Bunny,' I hissed to her.

'We both spoke to Bunny after you came to stay with me in Clapham with your friends. In fact it was Bunny who felt that it was time for Bob and me to talk.' See what I mean about parents being drama queens and hypocrites? I should have listened to Star all along.

'What do you mean, Bunny thought it was time? Time to throw your principles over and return to an oppressive man who can't pour his own granola, just because he's sold his horrible old stupid script?'

'No, we spoke because Honey had a bit too much to drink that weekend, and while you were all asleep she let slip about the fight with the drug dealers.'

'I knew Honey was behind this,' I shrieked, turning to Portia. 'I knew she'd try something like this! I knew it,' I railed.

'Knew what?' Portia asked, looking at me like I was

crazed. 'That she'd be instrumental in getting your parents back together?'

Sarah said, 'Darling, she wasn't being mean. She'd had a bit to drink and started opening up to me about her own parents' split. She told me how it had destroyed her life. She can be a really lovely girl when she's –'

'Drunk,' I spat.

'Please don't be bitter. It's a long story, but basically Bob and I are going to marriage guidance. We even talked about him going back to work –'

'I offered,' Bob added in his defence.

'Good man,' interjected Malcolm.

'Shut up, Malcolm,' I told him before turning to Bob. 'Oh, I bet you offered,' I said sarcastically. 'Offered in an emotionally blackmailing sort of way.'

'This is fantastic – the intrigue and dynamics behind a typical, middle-class American family.' Malcolm glowed. 'Are Americans always so against their parents reconciling?'

'Shut up, Malcolm,' Sarah said. 'He did offer to get a job, Calypso, and quite genuinely, but I couldn't let him. Not after all the time I'd put into supporting him to pursue his dream. Marriage is all about supporting one another through thick and thin, good times and bad. Bob had a dream and I wanted to support him in his creative endeavours,' Sarah explained as I stood there pressing my sabre deeper and deeper into the ground with all the force of my fury. The blade was bent to snapping point as I glared at my parents in teenage defiance.

'You've changed your tune,' I muttered.

'I knew he needed to finish it. I was just sick and tired of being neglected. It was complicated. I was conflicted. We both were, but relationships are full of misunderstandings. Bunny is a brilliant marriage therapist,' Sarah enthused.

'Bunny is a marriage therapist?' I cried in anguish.

'Who's Bunny?' asked Malcolm. 'She sounds fun.' But everyone ignored him.

'I know I vented some of my anger with Bob on you, darling,' Sarah admitted, patting my fencing mask, which was still tucked under my arm. 'It was wrong of me, but I was so angry about the sacrifices I'd made even though they were sacrifices I chose to make. I was conflicted.'

'So basically you used me? I was your emotional dartboard? I thought you hated Bob?'

'Oh no, I love your father, really. I never stopped loving him. You must know that. We made love all night last night, Calypso. It was just like the first time,' Sarah elaborated for me and anyone else in earshot.

Freds looked as horrified as Malcolm looked intrigued. Portia distracted Sister by launching into an animated discussion with her about her knitting. Bell End went puce in the face. Thank God that was when I was called to accept my cup.

Later, Adidas and Leon Paul marketing reps came to offer me sponsorship deals for the new kit I'd need to fence internationally and to cover my transport costs. Then Bell End started yakking on proudly and loudly about how I was a real GBR now and not a Great Badger

Rapist. But even then all I could think of was Bob and Sarah, having sex.

'Thanks for sharing your sex forensics, Mom,' I said later when the reps had left. I was hoping to put her in her proper parental place. Why do 'rents always have to make everything about them? Why do they always have to spoil their children's triumphs? This should have been *my* day, but now it was poisoned by an image that would be tattooed on my brain for the rest of my life. OK, so I was a bit pleased that they were sorting things out together, but I wished I hadn't already submitted that essay. Imagining my parents doing it, now that was *real* trauma.

Things got even worse after all the fanfare quieted down and we were leaving the building. Bob tweaked my cheek in front of everyone. 'See, my little Queen of the Doomsday Prophecies, didn't I tell you it would all work out?'

'Ah, let me think. No! You let me deal with Sarah's breakdown all on my own while you selfishly pursued your Big One. Then you swan in here, ruin my day and expect me to cheer because you've finally sold your script and can pay attention to your wife again.'

Bob ruffled my hair the way he knows I hate. 'Hey, don't underestimate Sarah. That slot she's been doing over here interviewing celebrities has been picked up at home by NBC. Besides, maybe one day when you ask me for a car you'll think differently,' he joked.

'I am not that materialistic,' I told him sharply, while secretly wondering what sort of car he'd let me have.

'Hey, give your old man a break. I knew I was almost

done when Sarah said she'd had enough. I was working on the last scene. And she'd made sacrifices for the script as well. I couldn't let her down. And don't forget, love is all about supporting one another's creative endeavours, Calypso.'

I shrugged him off as he tried to cuddle me, but he pulled me under his arm. 'I do give Sarah credit. In fact the script is called *To Sarah, with Love*.'

'They'll never let you keep that,' I told him, trying to suppress a smile. I could feel myself beginning to soften.

'It's written in the contract, Boojie,' he said. Oh this was great, now they were both reverting and referring to me in baby names.

Maybe Sister, Billy, Portia and Freds were right. Maybe one day I would forgive them. One thing was for sure, Bell End never would. Freds and Malcolm both tried to convince me that Sarah and Bob looked sweet together, but I know that was just because Bob had worked his charm on Freds by slapping him on the back and calling him 'buddy'. Buddy? Talk about sickening, but Freds seemed delighted with the term.

The worst of it came when they enveloped me in one of those gross family hugs Bob and Sarah have always insisted on.

'Isn't it marvellous,' Sister twittered. 'Marriage is a holy sacrament, after all. And two lovely people like you with a sweet little girl like Calypso for a daughter. Why, you're the perfect family.'

And that's when it hit me. I had just written an essay

about my suffering at the hands of this perfect family. An essay that had made Ms Topler weep with horror and wail with sorrow at the pain, pathos, torment and misery I had endured as an American girl packed off to a boarding school in England by the cruel Bob and self-involved Sarah. An essay, more importantly, that Ms Topler was convinced would win the competition and be plastered all over the pages of a national newspaper.

An essay that Bob and Sarah must absolutely never, ever read, because if they did, they would disown me and my happy family would be shot to smithereens. Passages I had written, which had seemed so poetic, inspired and heartfelt at the time I had written them, now seemed vitriolic and self-serving. Thank goodness Ms Topler was such a lousy English teacher and wouldn't know literature if it came and bit her on the nose. There was no way my miserable essay of personal suffering would have any chance of winning. Would it? Anyway, I had other far more pleasant things to dwell on.

'Freds loves me, Freds loves me,' I chanted to myself. And as if on cue, he put his arms around me. 'So, Princess Jelly Bean,' he whispered in my ear. 'I noticed there's nothing much going on behind the scoreboard . . . care to investigate?'

Glossary

FENCING TERMS

attack au fer: an attack that is prepared by deflecting an opponent's blade.

BNFA: British National Fencing Association.

bout: one single fight, usually lasting around six minutes.

compound attack: an attack incorporating two or more movements.

corps-à-corps: literally, body-to-body – physical contact between fencers during a bout (illegal in sabre).

disengagement: a way to continue attacking after being parried.

en garde: the 'ready' position fencers take before play.

épée: another weapon used in fencing.

FIE: Federation International D'escrime (International Fencing Association).

flèche: a way of delivering an attack whereby the attacker leaps to make the attack and then passes the opponent at a run. French word for 'arrow'.

flunge: an attack specific to sabre – a type of *flèche* attack in which the legs don't cross.

lamé: jacket made of interwoven wire and fabric.

parry: defensive move, a block.

parry of quinte: in sabre, a parry in which the blade is held above the head to protect from head cuts.

piste: a fourteen-metre-long combat area on which a bout is fought.

point: the tip of a weapon's blade.

pool: a group into which fencers are divided during preliminary rounds to assess ranking.

president: a registered referee or arbiter of the bout.

retire: retreat.

riposte: an offensive action made immediately after a parry of the opponent's attack.

sabre: The only cutting fencing blade. Points are scored both by hits made with the tip of the blade and by cuts made with the blade, but more commonly by cuts. The sabre target is everything above the leg, including the head and arms. For this reason the entire weapon, including the guard, registers hits on an electrical apparatus even though hitting the weapon's guard is not legal. This means the sabreur is totally wired -- unlike fencers using the other weapons. Before play begins, the sabreurs must check that all parts of their electric kit are working. This is done by the sabreurs tapping their opponents on the mask, the sabre, the guard and the metal jacket so that all hits will be recorded.

salle: fencing hall or club.

salute: once formal, now a casual acknowledgement of one's opponent and president at the start of a bout.

seeding: the process of eliminating fencers from their pools, based on the results of their bouts.

supermans: a fencing exercise – a holding stance used for warming up, so called because the fist is raised like Superman before he flies.

trompement: deception of the parry.

ENGLISH WORDS

arse: *derrière*. To make an arse of yourself means to embarrass yourself.

beaks: slang term for teachers at Eades.

blag: to talk your way into or out of something, or to fake something.

bless: an affectionate, sweet exclamation which, like all English words, can be used sarcastically.

blank/to be blanked: to not register someone; to look through them.

blue: blue paper given to write lines on; a minor punishment.

Body Shop Specials: empty Body Shop bottles filled with vodka.

bollocks: literally means testicles but used to mean useless, nonsense, ridiculous.

bottle out: chicken out, lose your nerve. 'Bottle' is another word for 'nerve,' so you can also 'lose your bottle'.

chav/chavie: A person defined by a common way of behaving or dressing. They have their favourite designer brands and love loads of bling. The opposite of posh or Sloaney.

common: slang for vulgar, of low social status, lacking charm or manners. Note: you can be rich and still be common.

crisps: potato chips.

cut: to ignore someone, to look right through them; see *blank/to be blanked*.

Daddy's plastic: parental credit cards.

DPGs: Daddy's Plastic Girls; girls who are defined by their limitless credit card privileges.

dressing down: telling off.

E-numbers: Artificial food additives.

en suite: bathroom attached to bedroom.

exeat: weekend at which pupils attending boarding school go home, usually every three weeks.

fag: cigarette.

fancy (v): to find someone attractive.

fit: Cute, hot, attractive. Girls and boys both use the word to describe the opposite sex. Note: a girl wouldn't refer to another girl as 'fit' – she'd say 'stunning'.

fruuping: all-purpose expletive.

gating: a punishment in which one is not permitted to leave the school grounds on weekends.

Glaswegian kiss: hitting someone on the nose with the lower brow – a blow that doesn't hurt the aggressor but renders the recipient stunned.

house mother or house mistress: female head of a boarding house

HRH: His (or Her) Royal Highness.

It Girl: society girl with a large media profile.

Jelly Babies: soft, brightly coloured sweets (candies) shaped like babies.

kit: equipment and outfit for specific event or activity.

knickers: panties. To get your knickers in a twist is to have a feverish panic.

Lady: daughter of a duke, marquis or earl; female life peers or wives of hereditary peers are also Ladies.

leg it: make a run for it.

Lower Sixth: year before the final year at school (age sixteen/seventeen).

mad: eccentric, crazy or unreasonable – out there.

madly: very, as in 'madly late'.

mobile: cell phone.

neck: to gulp, as in 'neck your vodka' (juice, etc.).

necking: as in neck; i.e., she was 'necking' her vodka, juice etc.

pash: pashmina.

piss-take/to take the piss: to tease, mimic or to make fun of someone, either maliciously or fondly; a joke.

plaster: a bandage.

pleb: short for 'plebeian' – a derogatory term suggesting lack of class.

plebbie (adj): for pleb (see above).

prat: idiot, fool.

pull: to make out, score, kiss, etc.

public school: exclusive boarding school.

rinse: to totally decimate your opponent in sport or debate.

rip: to ridicule, tease; equivalent to 'take the piss'.

rusticated: suspended from school without being given schoolwork to carry on with – meaning that on return, the pupil is further disadvantaged by having to catch up.

safe: 'OK'; an expression of agreement; see *sorted*.

slapper: a girl of loose morals.

Sloane: posh, snooty girl (named after Sloane Street and Square, an upscale area in London).

snog-age: (rhymes with 'corsage') to tongue kiss.

social: interschool dance (girls and boys).

sorted: an expression of approval; 'no problem'.

soz: sorry.

spliff: marijuana; a joint.

tomoz: tomorrow.

term: Three terms make up a school year: winter term is before Christmas; spring term is between Christmas and Easter; summer term is between Easter and the summer holiday.

ticked off: told off, reprimanded.

toff: snobby aristocrat.

torch: flashlight.

trackie bums: sweatpants.

trainers: sneakers.

trustafarian: trust fund girl with boho or artistic aspirations.

tuck: snack foods you are allowed to bring to boarding school; junk food.

tuck in: pig out.

wardrobe: closet.

wind up: to tease either gently or nastily.

wholemeal: whole wheat, used to describe decent, middle-class people.

Year: Girls start boarding at age 11 in Year Seven, and the 'Years' go up to Year Eleven (age 15–16). The final two years are referred to as the Lower Sixth and Upper Sixth (ages 16–17 and 18, respectively).

Acknowledgements

When I first conjured up the semi-fictional world of Saint Augustine's, I was inspired by my own school experiences and those of my children, especially Cordelia, who along with her stunning posse of friends and fans, has continued to inspire me throughout the first three books in the series. Shout outs and coronets to all the girls of Saint Mary's Ascot and the boys of Eton College. Your combination of style, wit, wisdom and worshipful looks are a credit to your generation!

Next, loads of curtsies for Zad Santospirito, my eldest son, whose stellar achievements on the piste, provided me with the material for Calypso's fencing scenes. Not only is he talented (and distressingly fit) but he is as wise and wily as Odysseus.

I also thank Eric Hewitson who drew the map so my characters wouldn't get lost in the vast grounds of Saint Augustine's. Mind you if I did get lost though, I would definitely want to be in the company of girls like Brenda Gardner at Piccadilly Press who encapsulates all that is best in teen fiction publishing. She knows about girl stuff – as does my editor Melissa Patey who sent me a frog to test drive. OK, so he didn't transform into a prince when I kissed him, but he does look fearfully sweet on my mantlepiece.

My final bow goes to my readers, especially the girls who write in to <u>askcalypso@calypsochronicles.com</u>. You totally rock!

www.piccadillypress.co.uk

☆ The latest news on forthcoming books

☆ Chapter previews

☆ Author biographies

☆ Fun quizzes

☆ Reader reviews

☆ Competitions and fab prizes

☆ Book features and cool downloads

☆ And much, much more . . .

Log on and check it out!

Piccadilly Press